Joshua shot her [barcode image] **for the auction."**

Silence filled the room.

Faith fiddled with the guest towels before she finally spoke. "If that's the only reason you've come, you're wasting your time. There's not going to be an auction."

Obviously, the woman was in denial. She'd lose her home and possibly her job. Maybe he could hire her—but really, why would she want to work for him? "What makes you say that?"

"I plan to contact the owner. I'll make him an offer, so an auction won't be necessary."

"And you have that kind of—" He bit his tongue, realizing he'd overstepped his bounds.

She grimaced. "Not right at the moment, but I'll get it. This property is way too important to me to let it go. I'll explain it to the owners—they'll understand."

If she only knew who she was up against, she'd realize she was fighting a losing battle. His father could care less about her family. He certainly didn't care about his own. "I wouldn't count on it."

Weekdays, **Jill Weatherholt** works for the City of Charlotte. On the weekend, she writes contemporary stories about love, faith and forgiveness. Raised in the suburbs of Washington, DC, she now resides in North Carolina. She holds a degree in psychology from George Mason University and a paralegal studies certification from Duke University. She shares her life with her real-life hero and number one supporter. Jill loves connecting with readers at jillweatherholt.com.

Books by Jill Weatherholt

Love Inspired

Second Chance Romance
A Father for Bella

A Father for Bella

Jill Weatherholt

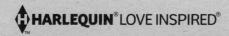

Recycling programs
for this product may
not exist in your area.

® LOVE INSPIRED BOOKS

ISBN-13: 978-1-335-42827-1

A Father for Bella

Copyright © 2018 by Jill Weatherholt

www.Harlequin.com

Printed in U.S.A.

Now faith is the substance of things hoped for,
the evidence of things not seen.
—*Hebrews* 11:1

To Derek, my forever hero.

Chapter One

"After a cold day on the slopes, come in for a warm stay at the Black Bear Inn and Ski Resort in Whispering Slopes, voted Shenandoah Valley's most popular inn." The radio advertisement warmed Joshua Carlson's heart as thoughts of his mother filled his mind. The Black Bear Inn—her favorite place. He had to save it.

He hit the turn signal on his silver luxury sedan. The rear wheels spun on a patch of ice as he continued up the steep driveway. A dusting of snow covered the manicured hedges lining the grounds. Puffs of smoke billowed from two massive chimneys and drifted toward the picturesque snow-capped mountains encompassing the property. Mahogany rocking chairs filled the wraparound porch on the two-story brick-and-stone home.

He zipped into the last available parking space. Good sign—the place was busy. No surprise there, because his father never owned anything that didn't make his wallet bulge.

Joshua stepped out of the car and pulled the crisp mountain air deep into his lungs. He'd always loved the smell of fresh pine. For the first time in months, his shoulders relaxed while he repeated slow and even breaths. The bitter divorce had taken a toll on him both physically and emotionally. He sauntered up the sidewalk, forgoing his luggage for now. He gripped the icy doorknob, wishing he'd worn gloves.

The pine floor gleamed as he crossed the threshold of the front entrance. He inhaled the citrus aroma filling the air. A winding staircase led to the second floor, where he spied a young couple sneaking a kiss—probably newlyweds. *I wonder how long that will last.* He shook away the negative thought. *Not every relationship ends with your first and only love walking out the door.*

"Bella! Where are you?"

With a jerk, he bolted to the back of the inn toward a woman's frantic scream.

"Bella!"

Joshua burst through the kitchen's swinging door and ran straight out the open back door. "What's going on?"

The woman jumped when he spoke. "It's my daughter, Bella. I can't find her." Tall and slender, dressed in blue jeans and a crisp white blouse, she raked her fingers through her wavy caramel brown hair spilling down her shoulders. She sprinted to the side of the building.

Joshua trailed behind, shoving his hands deep inside his coat pockets. It was early January and much too cold for her to go without a coat.

"Bella!" she shouted again and pressed her palms to the side of her head. "She asked if she could play outside with Plato. I told her to stay in sight." Her voice grew hoarse.

"Plato?"

"Her new puppy." The woman took off like a gazelle, stopping short at the edge of the forest. "It'll be dark soon." She cupped her hands to the sides of her mouth. "Bella! Answer me, please." She spun around and their eyes locked. "She's almost six and she's small for her age. And the forest is full of black bears and coyotes."

He swallowed hard, but the lump remained lodged in his throat. His hand grazed her forearm and she flinched at his touch. "Sorry— we'll find her, but we'll need some flashlights. It'll be dark soon."

"I can find her myself," she snapped.

"We'll find her sooner with both of us looking. Please, get me a flashlight, too." He sensed his presence made her feel like a mouse cornered by a barnyard cat, but there wasn't time to explain who he was and that he was only trying to help. The only things that mattered were that the sun was sinking fast and her daughter was somewhere in the thick forest.

Her left eyebrow arched. "I don't need—"

Boy, she was stubborn. "Yes, you do need my help and right now we're wasting daylight." He rubbed his hand across his cleanly shaved face.

She turned on her heel and bolted toward the open back door.

Joshua glanced to the sky. Daylight was fading as though on a dimmer switch.

The woman ran from the house with a flashlight in each hand, hesitating before passing it to him. "Here." For a second, her eyes narrowed as she scanned his face. "I'm Faith Brennan. Who are you?" She stepped back. "What are you doing back here?"

Of course she'd be alarmed. A strange man comes out of nowhere and wants her to go into the woods with him. "I'm Joshua Carlson— I'm a guest at the inn." He followed behind her as she tossed quick glances over her slender shoulder. Leaves crunched underneath his

Burberry leather shoes. Massive Fraser firs canopied the trampled path. Fraser fir, the only type of tree his father ever brought into their lavish Bethesda, Maryland, home at Christmas time. *They're the best tree, and we will only allow the best in this house.* He forced his father's voice from his head. "Is Bella familiar with the forest?"

"No. The path leads to the Shenandoah River. I've told her the force of the water is strong since we've had some heavy rains, but if Plato took off down the path, she'd go after him." Faith shook her flashlight and rammed it once against her thigh. "The batteries—they're going dead."

With a slight movement, his shoes slid on a patch of ice. "It'll be black as ink soon. Let me go ahead, I can move faster alone. You head back toward the inn, but keep calling her name." Thoughts of the path leading to the river propelled him deeper into darkness.

"Joshua!"

He came to a sudden halt and his feet skidded on the slushy leaves. "What is it?" Joshua turned and headed back in the direction he'd come.

Faith stood frozen. "It's one of her pink hair ribbons. She wanted her hair in ponytails this morning." Her hand flew over her mouth and tears erupted.

"Keep calling for her. I'll head toward the river." Faith's cries faded as he trekked farther into the forest. He turned on his flashlight and pointed it to the ground. *Your word is a lamp unto my feet and a light unto my path. Please keep Bella safe until we find her.*

Moments later, and deeper into the forest, the sound of rushing water filled his ears. The river was close. His pace quickened as tree branches smacked his face. His shoe caught on an exposed root and he went flying. His hands jammed into the frozen ground, breaking his fall. Springing to his feet, he wiped his hands down the front of his slacks.

"Mommy, help. It's so dark, and I'm cold."

At the sound of the tiny voice, Joshua halted in his tracks, his racing heart slowing. *She's safe, thank You. Your timing is always perfect.* "Bella, your mommy and I are here. Keep yelling so we know exactly where you are."

"My mommy says I shouldn't talk to strangers."

Relief washed over him as he moved closer, allowing her voice to guide him through the darkness. "She's right, but she's here, too."

"I can't see her."

"She's just up the path, Bella." He shoved

a branch from his face and darted toward the fearful voice. His breath caught in his throat when he spotted a mass of brown sugar curls on one side of her head and a ponytail tied with a pink ribbon on the other side. She was crouched on the cold path, her face snuggled against a snow-white puppy.

"Who are you?" She pushed the curls from her face to reveal the biggest blue eyes he'd ever seen. "Where's my mommy?"

Her voice, sweet as honeysuckle, clutched hold of his heart. "She's here. I'm Joshua, a guest at the inn. I heard your mommy yelling for you when I arrived." He reached for her hand to help her off the frozen ground.

She kissed the top of Plato's head and sprung to her feet, holding the puppy tight. "She always worries. She thinks I'm still a baby."

At the sound of leaves rustling and twigs snapping along the path, Joshua turned and saw the girl's mother.

"You'll always be my baby," Faith proclaimed and pulled Bella into her arms, smothering her face with kisses. "You know you're not supposed to wander into the forest. We've talked about the dangers."

"Mommy, you're squishing Plato." Bella nuzzled her face into the white ball of fur. "I had

to. Plato chased a squirrel. He can't be alone—
he's too little."

Faith swiped a tear. "So are you, young lady.
Now promise me, no more venturing off alone."

He studied mother and daughter. The discernible love between Faith and Bella brought
a slow smile to Joshua's lips as it reminded him
of his own relationship with his mother before
she went to be with the Lord. "You must get
your striking blue eyes from your daddy."

Faith's face turned to stone.

He glanced toward Bella. Her lower lip quivered. His chest constricted. What had he said?
A squirrel scurried past, stirring the frozen
leaves.

Bella squirmed loose from her mother's
arms. On the ground, she stepped toward him.
"I don't have a daddy anymore." She looked
up, and the flashlight caught a beacon of hope
in her eyes. "How did you know he had blue
eyes? Did you know him?"

Bile rose in his throat and he shook his head.
"No, I'm sorry." He cupped his hand under her
chin. "I didn't know your daddy."

Her shoulders dropped, and she kicked the
ground with her neon-pink tennis shoe. A
northerly gust of wind tousled her hair. "Oh."

Faith cleared her throat and picked up the
dog. She reached for her daughter's hand. "We

better start back." She took a few steps forward. Bella pulled loose and stepped toward Joshua.

His breath was slow and easy when she placed her tiny hand inside of his own.

"I want to walk with Mr. Joshua. He smells like peppermint."

He eyed Faith, who hesitated, but then gave him a cautious nod. "Peppermint is my favorite chewing gum." He smiled and gave Bella a wink.

"Mine, too," she said with a giggle. "How long are you staying at the inn?" She skipped along at his side with one ponytail still intact.

Joshua paused when he noticed Faith turn her head the tiniest bit. Was she curious, too? "Well, it all depends."

"On what?"

He laughed. "I have some business to take care of."

"What kind of business?"

"Bella!" Faith stopped in her tracks and whirled around. "What have I told you about asking so many questions?"

The little girl bit down on her pouted lip. "I'm sorry."

As they neared the edge of the forest, the light from the inn flashed along Bella's rosy cheeks. She gave her mother a sly glance. "Are you married, Mr. Joshua?"

"Bella! That's enough. Take Plato inside and see if Mrs. Watson needs your help with dinner." She placed the puppy in her daughter's arms.

"Okay…but will you make some hot chocolate for me and Mr. Joshua?"

Faith rubbed the back of her neck. "Well—"

Joshua sensed the last thing she wanted to do was have hot chocolate with a complete stranger. "That's nice of you to offer, Bella, but I should get checked in."

"Please, Mommy."

The two grown-ups exchanged a quick glance, and he nodded.

"Maybe—now go on inside." Faith turned to Joshua as Bella darted through the back door. Her forehead puckered. "I apologize for my daughter's rude behavior. I don't know what's gotten into her today."

He shook his head. "You don't need to apologize. That's what's great about kids—they're so inquisitive."

Faith paused and raised an eyebrow. "Oh, so you have children?" Her hand flew to her mouth. "Listen to me, now I sound like Bella."

"No, I have a lot of friends with kids." Him? A father? That couldn't happen—especially when his wife didn't want to raise a family together. "So, do you work at the inn?"

She nodded as they headed through the back door and into the kitchen. His stomach rumbled at the smell of baking bread. "Yes, I'm the manager. I started working here after—ah, about four years ago."

Joshua noticed her hesitation, but didn't want to pry. What he did want to find out, without raising suspicion, was how successful the inn was. The last thing he wanted was for his father to get wind of his plan. "It seems like a great place to work. By the looks of the parking lot you must stay busy." He scanned the brightly painted yellow walls and realized his father hadn't played a role in the decorating. He hated yellow. *Green, the color of money— it's the only color that matters.* Joshua cringed at the memory.

Faith reached for a red cable sweater draped over the back of the oak chair. "Yes, especially during the ski season. The inn has five rooms, each with its own private bathroom. It's a big draw." She pulled a saucepan from the maple cupboard and placed it on the six-burner gas stovetop. "I take it you ski?" She grabbed the milk carton from the double-sided stainless-steel refrigerator.

He did ski, but it wasn't the reason for his visit. "Yes, I've skied since I was a boy." He turned at the sound of Bella as she walked into the kitchen whistling "Mary Had a Little Lamb." The lone ponytail was now released, freeing a mass of messy curls.

"Are you going to have hot chocolate, too, Mr. Joshua?"

He glanced toward Faith while she poured the milk into the pan.

She turned, wearing a pasted-on smile. "After coming to our rescue, it's the least we can do." She stirred in three heaping tablespoons of chocolate powder. "After we drink this, we'll get you settled in your room. I'm sure you're tired from the drive."

She was suddenly strictly business, which was fine by him. He hadn't come to Whispering Slopes to make friends, especially with a woman as attractive as Faith. "Actually, it's only a little over two hours from where I live in Bethesda, Maryland. It's just outside of Washington, DC."

Bella pounced into one of the four stools lining the earth-toned granite island situated in the center of the kitchen. "That's our capital." She twirled her finger around a loose curl and smiled. "That's where you live? Cool!"

Joshua slid into the empty stool next to her as he caught a whiff of the sweet cocoa. "You're right, Bella, it is our capital. It was a great place to grow up. What else do you know about Washington?"

She gazed up toward the pendant lighting, pursing her lips. "Well, the President lives there, and the pandas at the zoo—they're from China. Have you ever been there?"

His mind flooded with warm memories of trips to the zoo with his mother. She had always been there for him...the one person who'd loved him right. His father could never spare an afternoon for his family. "Oh, yes, many times. My favorite part is the ape house."

"I love monkeys, too." Bella giggled. "Mommy, can we go to that zoo sometime?"

Faith poured the hot chocolate into the first of three oversize red-and-white mugs. "Maybe someday we will. Now, who wants marshmallows?"

Bella bounced in her stool. "I do, I do! I want the mini ones." She turned to Joshua. Her eyes, the size of walnuts, tripped his heart. "Do you like the small ones, too, Mr. Joshua?"

"Yes, but only five, please."

Her head slightly tilted. "How come?"

"It's my favorite number."

"Mommy, can I have five?" She grinned at Joshua. "It's my favorite number, too."

Faith raised an eyebrow. "But you always

like them overflowing in the cup. You love the marshmallow mustache."

"Just five." She turned her gaze back to Joshua.

Her mother shrugged her shoulders. "Okay, then."

Joshua watched while Faith filled each mug with the rich, creamy chocolate. She counted the marshmallows and tossed a few extra into her cup. She peered at Joshua and her cheeks reddened.

"Hot chocolate just isn't the same unless it leaves a marshmallow mustache." She slid a mug in front of him.

He took a sip and ran his tongue along his lips, savoring the sweet marshmallow residue. When he spied Faith doing the same, his heartbeat quickened—she sure was cute. Joshua pulled his shoulders back and looked away. He didn't need any distractions.

Seeing guests come and go at the Black Bear was normal for Faith, but she wasn't in the mood to entertain the guests this evening. Her mind was preoccupied after she'd read the disturbing news about the inn, just minutes before Bella wandered off. Her stomach knotted as she thought about what could have happened. She was thankful Joshua had arrived when he did.

He was certainly striking. At five feet and eight inches, she'd always considered herself tall, but next to him, she felt tiny. He'd be about six foot three, she guessed. It was difficult not to stare at him, with his closely cut dark hair and chiseled features, but his looks were a good reason why she needed to keep her distance. Obviously, he'd captured Bella's heart. Most nights, Faith overheard her daughter saying her prayers. Bella always prayed for a daddy and a new husband for her mommy.

"Mommy, did you hear me?"

She jumped at the sound of Bella's voice. "I'm sorry, sweetie, what did you say?"

"Can Mr. Joshua come to our house for dinner tonight?" Bella gazed at her newfound hero with starry eyes.

Faith bit the inside of her cheek and glanced toward Joshua, who appeared completely at ease with the question. "Bella, don't be silly. We've taken up enough of his time. He hasn't even checked into his room." She noticed the empty mug. "Speaking of, Mrs. Watson typically checks in our guests, but if you're finished, I can take care of that."

Bella hopped off her stool. Plato, who'd been asleep on a fluffy brown pillow by the back door, jumped up. His toenails scrabbled as he scurried along the hardwood floor, his tail moving like windshield wipers in a driving rainstorm. Bella grabbed Joshua's hand. "I can show him!"

He smiled at Bella before turning to Faith. "I appreciate your hospitality, but I don't want to keep you from going home." He glanced at his watch. "It's almost dinnertime, and isn't tonight a school night, Bella?" He rubbed the top of her head.

Faith walked to the sink. "Yes, it is." She poured the rest of her hot chocolate down the drain and rinsed the cup under some warm water. "Let's get you settled into your room." She dried her hands on the striped dishtowel and flung it on the granite counter.

"Oh, man, school ruins everything, even if I'm only in kindergarten." Bella scooped Plato into her arms and kissed the top of his head. "I'm going to go watch Mr. Watson. He's building something in the basement."

"Don't bother him while he's working. We'll head home as soon as I get Mr. Joshua checked in."

"I won't bother him." She skipped out of the room with her dog tight in her arms, whistling a random tune.

Joshua turned to Faith and smiled. "You've got your hands full with that one."

"You're not kidding. I think the child was born whistling."

They headed out of the kitchen and into the foyer. Chatter from the dining room echoed across the foyer. The aroma of tangy mustard and brown sugar tickled her nose. Home-style meat loaf smothered in onions was Chef Michael's specialty, and Faith's favorite.

"The Black Bear must have a great chef. That's quite a crowd." He pointed toward the dining room. "And the food…it smells wonderful."

Her heart sank as the newspaper article she'd read before Bella took off seeped back into her mind. Would Michael lose his job? Would she lose hers? And what about her home? The inn couldn't be going up for auction out of nowhere, but according to the paper that was the owner's plan. Why hadn't she been told? As the manager for four years, she should have been informed.

She couldn't think about that—not now. "Yes, Michael came from a popular restaurant in New York City about three years ago. He gave up the frantic pace of city life. We're grateful we hired him. He knows how to bring in the crowds."

"They're not all guests, are they?"

She shook her head. "No, we've got a lot of the locals who love his food."

Where would everyone eat after the inn was sold? The paper said there were rumors of an upscale resort and condos. What would happen to the quaint cottage she rented on the property? Bella called it their gingerbread house. It'd been their home since the fire.

Faith stepped behind a mahogany counter and tapped her fingers on the keyboard. "Oh, I see you have reservations for four weeks." Her head tilted to the side. "Our guests normally don't stay that long. Many are weekend warriors who come up to hit the slopes. You must be a great skier."

He examined his fingernails. "I'm okay, I guess."

Faith scrolled through the information and took notice of the Bethesda address he'd mentioned earlier. Her best friend from high school had graduated from George Washington University in DC. Real estate in the surrounding area wasn't cheap. She wondered what Joshua did for a living, but didn't want to appear nosy by asking. "It's nice you're able to take so much time off from work."

He nodded and pulled his credit card from an eel-skin wallet. "I assume you take this? Or would you rather have a different kind?"

Faith grabbed the card and swiped it through the machine. "This is fine."

The click of the equipment printing the receipt filled the air while they waited.

"Earlier, I heard an advertisement for the inn on the radio. Do you do any other form of advertising?" He slipped his credit card into his wallet.

He was certainly curious about the business. Perhaps he was only making conversation. "Not really. Word of mouth works well for the Black Bear." She tugged the receipt from the machine and slid it across the counter for his signature.

She stole a quick glance at the signature—Carlson. Why did the name seem familiar? "Do you have any family in the area?" She waited for his answer as he pulled a pack of peppermint gum from his pocket.

"No, my family's all from Bethesda." He extended the pack of gum in front of her. "Would you like a piece?"

Her cheeks warmed as she accepted the offer. "Thank you." She peeled away the foil and slid the cool stick on her tongue. Peppermint had always been her favorite, too.

"What about you? Any family in the area?"

"Only my twin sister, Joy, and she's a school-teacher here in Whispering Slopes."

"Joy and Faith… I like that, and twins, too. When I was a kid, I always thought it would be great to have an identical twin. You know, to play tricks on your teachers and other kids." He flashed a smile.

She forced her eyes away from his rugged good looks. Why did he make her so nervous? "We're not identical twins. Except for our hair color, we're nothing alike, but we're closer than any twins you'll ever meet." She rolled the gum wrapper between her fingers into a tight ball, anxious to get home.

"I guess that made it easier on your parents. Do they live in the area?"

Ready for him to leave, but not wanting to be rude, she answered. "They died in a car accident while driving to the Outer Banks of North Carolina to celebrate their anniversary." She paused when a shiver ran down her spine. "Joy and I were only two years old, so our grandparents raised us—here in this house." The sound of her parents' voices or the feel of their touch was something she couldn't remember. All that remained were a few boxes stuffed with crinkled photographs. Except for the past four years, she felt she'd barely had roots or a home—another reason why she couldn't lose the inn.

"I'm sorry. I didn't mean to reopen old wounds." His voice cracked.

Faith shook her head. "No, it's okay." But it really wasn't. Sharing pieces of her personal life with a strange man—what was she thinking? It was wrong. "Listen to me rambling on. You're probably exhausted." She stepped out from behind the counter with his room key in her hand. "Do you need help with your luggage?"

"No, thank you. I can handle it." He turned and headed toward the front door.

With a stack of credit card receipts, Faith scuttled to her office, which was located off the foyer. The massive cherry desk that faced a floor-to-ceiling window provided her with an amazing daytime view, especially on snowy winter days. She slipped behind her desk and opened the lateral file drawer. She fingered through the manila file folders before placing the receipts inside. As she started to push the drawer closed, her eyes locked on a folder labeled "Our Dream." She slammed the drawer shut. *Our dream, baby—we both wanted it so bad. You'd still be alive if we'd gone after it sooner.*

Her thoughts shifted when Joshua stepped into the foyer carrying a large black suitcase, along with a leather briefcase. Perhaps this was an extended trip for pleasure and business. She pushed in the lock before pulling it shut and headed toward the door. "Let's go upstairs. Your room is the first one on the right."

The sound of their footsteps echoed as they climbed the winding oak staircase. Once at the door, she slid the key into the doorknob and pushed it open.

"Wow! I wasn't expecting such a large room." Joshua smiled and stepped inside. His gaze stopped at the stone fireplace. "And it has its own fireplace—very nice."

She flipped the light switch. The recessed lighting provided a warm glow throughout the room. "This is the largest of our five rooms. The other four are much smaller." Heat filled her face. "Actually, it's our honeymoon suite."

"I take it there're no honeymooners coming into town the next four weeks."

She watched Joshua set his suitcase down on the luggage rack.

"This office space is perfect." He placed his briefcase on top of the desk.

Faith flipped the plantation shutters closed. "We used to have it arranged as a sitting room, but one suggestion that continued to come up in the guest surveys was they'd like a workspace. I suppose with the internet, people don't know how to unplug from the office anymore, even on their honeymoon."

He nodded. "I think the room is perfect, and it smells so outdoorsy."

"It's pine. Usually for the honeymooners, we use lavender. We made a quick adjustment for you." She tucked a piece of hair behind her ear. "I'm going to let you get settled." She handed over the key and pointed toward the desk. "The number for Mr. and Mrs. Watson is on that information sheet. They live on the premises in a spare room, off from the dining area. You'll probably meet them when you go down to dinner. If you need anything, please give them a call."

Faith reached for the doorknob and turned around. "I almost forgot. Dinner's served until nine thirty. I'm sure you're starved."

"Actually, I am kind of hungry. I'll definitely order the meat loaf. It smelled like my mother's recipe." He smiled.

"Yes, Michael's Thursday night special is a crowd-pleaser. He makes terrific garlic mashed potatoes, too." Her stomach grumbled. She hadn't eaten anything since lunch, and that was only a small bowl of vegetable soup.

Joshua stepped toward the door and extended his hand. "Thank you for your help checking in. I appreciate it."

She hesitated before reaching for his hand. "It's part of my job. Besides, I'm the one who should thank you."

"For what?"

Her gaze met his. "For finding Bella… I get sick to my stomach thinking what could have happened."

"She's safe now, that's what matters." He ran his hands down the front of his slacks. "Speaking of, you be safe driving home. On my ride here, I spotted several deer darting across the road."

Faith smiled. "I don't have to drive anywhere. My house is on the property."

Joshua began to cough and clutched his hand to his throat.

She reached for his forearm. "Are you okay?"

He nodded. "Yes, I'm fine. I swallowed my gum, that's all." His face reddened. "Did you say you live here—on the property of the Black Bear?"

"Yes. We live in a two-bedroom cottage." Faith noticed his coloring had turned from red to pale in a manner of seconds. "It's adjacent to the back of the inn."

He gave a quick nod and grabbed the doorknob. With a swift jerk, he pulled the door wide open—her clue to leave. She turned and walked through the door. When it slammed behind her, she realized neither had said goodbye. Odd. The new guest had been so friendly earlier. Why did he seem rattled to learn that she and Bella lived on the grounds of the inn?

Chapter Two

Joshua closed the door fast, but it didn't release the guilt that gripped him. The ticking wall clock in the office space caused his thoughts to race. She lived on the property? He didn't recall seeing a house.

Discovering that Faith had lived at the inn after her parents were killed was bad enough, but being a landlord wasn't part of his plan. How could he evict a young mother and her child? There were so many other things that needed his attention prior to the auction, but this was a huge, unexpected curveball.

He strolled toward the clock and took it off the wall. Carefully, he removed the batteries and remounted it. He'd never liked the sound of time passing him by.

As he admired the Bob Timberlake painting hanging adjacent to the stacked-stone fireplace, his cell phone chirped. Without looking at the screen, he pulled it from his back pocket. "Hello, Joshua Carlson speaking."

"Josh, hey, it's Steve-o." Steve Hayes, his best friend from Georgetown University.

His voice brought a smile to Joshua's face. "Steve-o, it's great to hear from you—it's been a while."

"It's my fault, man. I've been working in London for the past four months. I had to set up a new network system for one of our customers. The hours have been brutal."

"No problem. I know you tech guys work around the clock."

A brief silence hung in the air.

"I just heard about your mom, Josh. I'm really sorry. I wish I'd known. I would have flown back for the funeral."

First the cancer diagnosis and within six months, she was with the Lord. It was hard to believe a month had passed since he'd kissed her cheek and held her hand for the last time. "Don't worry about it. I should have called you, but it was a small service. You know how my father is, always trying to keep family business hush-hush."

"How's he doing? Despite his ways, I know he loved your mom."

"Yes, he did. I think it's been tough for him,

but we haven't talked since the funeral…we hardly spoke then. He's still angry at me for quitting my job at his firm." He didn't want to dump the gory details on his friend, but the truth was that his father had disowned his only son. "I did hear from Melissa."

"So, she's still handling your legal affairs?"

"Yeah, she said my dad's attorney told her that my dad's getting rid of anything that reminds him of my mother."

"That must be tough on him."

"He's even selling the businesses. The hotels and inns they'd owned together are either for sale or going up for auction." He paused. He could trust Steve to keep his plan under wraps. "That's why I'm in Whispering Slopes."

"Whispering Slopes—the ski resort in the Shenandoah Valley? The Black Bear Inn, wasn't that your mother's favorite place?"

He smiled. Steve had always been a good listener. "Yes, it was. My father's putting it up for auction and I plan to make an offer. I've got a healthy nest egg saved, as well as my trust account. Hopefully it will cover the cost. There's no way I'll let strangers take over the inn. It meant too much to my mother." He paused as the ache of losing her bubbled to the surface. "It's all I have left of her."

"I understand. Do you think he's too angry at you for leaving his firm to gift the place to you?"

Joshua slid into the leather club chair next to the fireplace. "Angry isn't the word for it." Despite Steve being his best friend, it was tough to admit his own father thought he was a loser. He glanced out the window. The outdoor spotlight exposed a gathering of seven white-tailed deer on the grounds below.

The silence lingered for a couple of seconds. Joshua hadn't meant to make his friend uncomfortable "It's all good. I'm going to buy this inn and the surrounding property. My plan is to redevelop it and make it a five-star resort." Although Faith and her daughter would present a bigger problem than he anticipated, he wasn't backing down—he couldn't. "It's going to be the best resort on the East Coast."

"I have no doubt it will. But one thing, how will you keep your father from finding out about your plan?"

Joshua straightened his shoulders. "His lawyers will handle everything since he's out of the country right now. Besides, Melissa will place the bid on my behalf. I'll be behind the scenes, so she'll handle everything. Dad will never know who bought it until long after the deal is sealed. By then, there won't be anything he can do." At least he hoped there wouldn't be.

Steve chuckled. "It sounds like you've got a good plan." He paused for a moment. "I'm surprised Melissa is still working as your attorney. After all the years she pined over you, you married Jessica, her best friend. I figured she'd moved on."

Joshua had never tried to lead Melissa on. They'd known each other since high school and only dated briefly during their junior year. She was a little too high-strung for his taste. Plus, God wasn't first in her life. "Well, she knows her stuff when it comes to the law."

Before ending the call, the two friends promised to make an effort to talk more often. Joshua hung up and walked toward the window. It was spitting snow. Jessica never liked the snow. She preferred white sandy beaches and crystal-blue water. His stomach turned as he thought of her. He'd believed he'd known her, especially since they'd dated for three years before they were married. But as soon as she found out he'd quit his job, she'd walked. Right into more money. *Five years of marriage and she left me for some rich guy.* He mauled his face with his free hand, picturing her on an island in the Caribbean.

He didn't feel so hungry after all.

* * *

The following morning, after a shower and shave, Joshua donned a black polo shirt and tan slacks before zipping downstairs to the dining room for a quick breakfast. After seeing the snow last night, he couldn't wait to hit the slopes. He'd had a restless night thinking about Faith's home on the property. He needed to clear his mind.

He relaxed his shoulders when he stepped inside the dining room and noticed it wasn't nearly as crowded as last night. He could deal with out-of-town guests, but the locals were more inclined to ask questions.

He strolled through the dining area. Red cedar beams extended along the ceiling. A large stone fireplace in the center of the room emitted an orange glow, providing a warm and cozy focal point. The aroma of sizzling bacon caused his stomach to rumble.

Sliding into the empty table next to the large windows covering the entire back wall, he knew why this had been his mother's favorite place. The panoramic views of the slopes were incredible. Bringing the outside in was a very nice touch…this was something he'd have to keep in mind during the renovations.

Moments later, a petite woman with hair as white as cotton approached him. With a stubby orange pencil tucked behind her ear, she carried a pot of coffee—just what he needed.

"Well, good morning. Joshua, isn't it? I'm Mrs. Watson. I'm sorry I missed you at dinner last night." She wiped her hands down the front of her red-and-white-checked apron and extended her right hand.

After learning Faith lived on the property and thoughts of Jessica, he'd lost his appetite. "I decided to turn in early."

"Bella told me Faith got you settled into your room." She flashed a toothy grin. "You certainly impressed our little girl. She went on and on about how you rescued her in the woods as though you were a superhero."

She sure could talk. Taking advantage of her pause, he stood and shook her hand. "Yes, I'm Joshua. I'm not so sure about the superhero bit, but I'm glad I arrived when I did."

Mrs. Watson released a heavy sigh. "Amen!"

"I'm anxious to get out on the slopes this morning."

Mrs. Watson filled his cup to the brim with a piping hot dark-roast blend. "Conditions are excellent this morning. We picked up several inches of snow overnight."

"I noticed it coming down at a pretty good clip before I went to bed last night." He glanced toward the lobby and saw Faith dressed in a lemon-lime ski suit.

Mrs. Watson turned and pointed. "Faith's getting ready to go out with some of the guests, if you're interested. She organizes all types of outdoor activities for our snow lovers."

He preferred to ski alone, but since he wasn't familiar with the slopes, it might be a good idea to go with a group. Plus, it would be a good opportunity to get some valuable information about the resort from Faith. "It sounds like fun. Are you sure she won't mind another person?" His eyes shifted to the lobby, but she was gone.

"Oh, no, she loves when the guests participate. Why don't I put in your breakfast order while you go let her know you want to join the group? They'll be heading out within the hour."

Joshua smiled. "Perfect."

"You know, she's quite the skier. She's won several big competitions in the state."

"Really?" He wasn't too surprised. She had an athletic build, like a runner.

"She's a great instructor if you're just learning."

"I've been skiing since I was a boy, so I won't need lessons." His stomach grumbled. "Now, about my order—I'll have a cheese omelet, two slices of toast and some of that delicious-smelling bacon."

She scribbled on her pad and stuck the pencil behind her ear.

"Faith should be in her office." She turned and scurried toward the kitchen.

Joshua grabbed his coffee and headed toward the lobby. The young couple he'd seen yesterday when he'd first arrived headed out the front door, each carrying a sled. He liked the idea of the inn offering many outdoor activities for its guests. He'd do the same, but his plans would be on a much grander scale.

Although the door to Faith's office was open, he gently knocked.

She looked up with a half smile that quickly disappeared.

He gripped his cup with both hands. "I'm sorry to disturb you."

She rested her pen on the desk and stood. "Don't be silly—come in."

He hesitated for a moment before entering her office. Her ski pants swooshed as she crossed the room to meet him halfway. A faint scent of his ex-wife's favorite cologne tickled his nose. Somehow it smelled different on Faith. Better.

"What can I do for you?"

"Mrs. Watson mentioned you were taking a group out skiing this morning."

Faith crossed her arms across her chest. "Yes... I am."

"Do you have room for one more?"

She paused for a moment. A woodpecker drilled on the oak tree outside the window.

"Of course. Will you need equipment?"

He never skied without his own gear. It would be like using someone else's toothbrush. "No, I brought my stuff. Remember, I did come for some skiing, too." She didn't need to know his business motives—at least not now.

"Okay. We're heading out at ten o'clock. Does that work for you?"

He spied a cuckoo clock on the wall, but it read four o'clock. He pointed toward it. "Looks like you need to wind the clock."

She turned and shook her head. "It belonged to my grandmother. I can't stand the sound of a ticking clock."

His lips parted to share with her their similar dislike, but he decided against it. No sense getting personal. He checked his watch. "That'll work. I just have to eat breakfast and change clothes."

"That's fine. We'll all meet in the lobby at ten." She stepped toward her desk, but stopped short and turned. "We'll ski a black diamond course today. Do you have experience with that level of difficulty?"

Joshua nodded. "Of course I do."

Shortly after ten o'clock, Faith squirmed in the chairlift as it climbed the slope. She wasn't happy she'd ended up sharing a chair with Joshua, but since the others were coupled up, it only made sense.

"So how long have you been skiing?"

She wasn't in the mood for small talk, not with an eligible bachelor. Was he single? There was no ring on his finger. But with his good looks he probably had women throwing themselves at him. What did she care anyway? "All of my life. When you grow up in Whispering Slopes, they slap skis on your feet as soon as you start to walk."

He laughed as he scanned the view. "It's spectacular up here. When I was a kid, I always felt like I was riding to Heaven when I went up on the chairlift." He paused and looked up toward the sky. "I remember thinking God could hear me better since I was up higher."

Faith had felt that way once upon a time, but not anymore. Not since God took away the only man she'd ever loved.

The chair stopped with a jerk despite being only halfway to the top.

Great.

This wasn't how she'd planned on spending her morning. Stuck on the slopes and talking about God. With another abrupt movement, the chair continued its climb. She released a sigh of relief.

Joshua turned and flashed a crooked smile. "Phew. For a minute there, I thought we'd be up here for a while and forced to continue this strained conversation."

Reaching the top of the mountain, they disembarked and waited for the others. Since everyone was an advanced skier, she'd brought them to the Black Bear's most difficult slope, the Matterhorn.

With the group gathered in a circle, Faith adjusted her goggles. "The report said the trails are a little icy this morning, so everyone use caution. If you choose to break off from the group, make sure you check in with me when you return to the inn, so everyone is accounted for. Even though you're all advanced, I think you'll find the Matterhorn to be quite a challenge. Be safe, but most important, have fun."

Faith watched as the couples headed down the slope, breaking off as she'd expected.

"You ready?"

She flinched at the sound of his smooth voice and the smell of sweet peppermint. "Ready?"

"Yeah, unless you plan to stand here admiring the view for the rest of the day. What do you say—wanna ski together?" Joshua suggested as he adjusted his goggles.

The sooner she got down to the bottom and away from him, the better. "Sure, let's go."

She dug her poles in the ground and pushed. The cold air exploded in her face as she glided down the slope. This was where she was happiest. Swishing down the slopes, she felt as though she was leaving all of the hurt and pain behind. Too bad it always waited for her at the bottom.

Several minutes into the run, she spied Joshua off to her left. He whooshed down the hill with the ease of a professional. Her stomach lurched when she hit an icy spot and almost took a spill. Seconds later, she watched as Joshua's poles went flying into the air and he was suddenly tumbling down the slope straight toward a cluster of trees. She made a quick turn with her skis. A wave of snow swooshed in the air before she came to a dead stop. She pushed forward in his direction—but it was too late. Joshua had hit the trees and was lying motionless in the snow.

Crouching by his side, she removed her skis and dropped to her knees. "Joshua! Can you hear me?" Her heart pounded through her jacket. She reached into her pocket and grabbed her phone to call for help.

"Black Bear Inn, can I help you?" Thankful Mrs. Watson answered on the first ring, Faith struggled to catch her breath.

"Mrs. Watson—it's Faith. There's been an accident up on Matterhorn at marker five. Can you call Doug? He and Jerry will need to bring the stretcher. And please, hurry. Mr. Carlson is unconscious."

Faith ended the call and stuffed her cell into her pocket. She reached toward Joshua and carefully removed his goggles, not wanting to move him the slightest bit. "Can you hear me?" His eyes remained closed.

Within minutes, the rumble of the approaching snowmobile echoed up the slope. "Hang on, help is coming."

She rubbed her wet glove across her forehead. Why had she allowed him to come without seeing his ability as a skier, first? She'd been out with the others in the group and knew they were qualified to ski a challenging run. She held her breath as Doug and Jerry gently lifted Joshua and placed him on the stretcher.

Thirty minutes later, she was pacing the floor at Valley Memorial Hospital. The fluorescent lighting buzzed overhead, triggering her memory. She had to get out of here. And fast. Beads of perspiration surfaced on her fore-head. She took a sip of the bitter coffee and grimaced. Everything about this place made her stomach queasy.

"Faith!"

She turned and spotted Mrs. Watson racing down the hall. For a sixty-eight-year-old woman, she was in great shape.

"I got here as fast as I could. How's Mr. Carlson?"

Amazingly, she wasn't even out of breath. "He's with the doctor now. They're doing a CT scan." Faith had been relieved once Doug and Jerry got Joshua to the bottom of the slope and the ambulance had been waiting. "He regained consciousness on the way here. Hopefully he'll be okay."

Mrs. Watson pulled off her coat and flung it on a nearby chair. "So what happened?"

All the way to the hospital, Faith had recalled the last few minutes on the trail. "I'm not sure. One minute he was skiing like a professional, and then he went down. He must have hit some ice."

"Well, thank God you were with him. What if he'd been up there by himself?"

Faith had the exact thought. That trail didn't get as much use as the intermediate and beginner's slopes. Who knows how long he could have lain up there? She shook off the negative thought.

The two women paced the floor for the next thirty minutes. They both turned at the sound of approaching footsteps.

"Hello, Faith, Mrs. Watson." The tall, slender red-haired man smiled before slipping his wire-framed glasses on.

"Hello, Dr. Maxwell," they responded in unison.

He extended his hand to Faith. His grip was firm. "I understand Mr. Carlson is a guest at your inn."

"That's correct. He checked in with us yesterday. Is he going to be okay?" It had been four years since she'd been in this hospital. Her knees weakened. The sooner she could get out of here the better.

"He's regained consciousness and gave us his father's number, but we weren't able to reach him. Mr. Carlson said it was okay if we talk with you about his condition, since his father probably wouldn't call back."

Faith lifted an eyebrow. Odd. What kind of father wouldn't return a phone call concerning his injured son?

The doctor skimmed the papers on his clipboard. "He's very fortunate he didn't sustain any broken bones. He's got a mild concussion and will need to be monitored closely for a day or two."

"Oh, no problem whatsoever, Doctor. Faith and I can take care of him."

What? Why was Mrs. Watson so quick to volunteer her services? If she wanted to care for him, fine, but there was no way Faith would play nurse. She had enough on her plate. "Uh… can't he stay here? Things are really hectic right now." Her world was about to turn upside down if she didn't figure out a plan to place a bid on the inn. She couldn't lose it…it was all the security she and Bella had in their life.

Mrs. Watson stepped forward. "Nonsense, Faith. With your medical background, we can handle the inn and Mr. Carlson. After all, it's the least we can do for a guest who's planning such a long stay."

"Exactly what I was thinking. With four years of medical school under your belt, you're more than qualified," Dr. Maxwell said. "Besides, he's contributing to our local economy and it's important we give special attention to our out-of-town visitors. We want to keep them coming back, don't we?"

What was happening here? Faith raked her fingers through the back of her thick hair. Yes, she had completed medical school. She'd just begun her residency when her entire world collapsed around her. Medicine was part of her past—and exactly where it would stay.

The overhead intercom filled the hall with static, paging Dr. Maxwell. "I have to get going. I'll keep Mr. Carlson overnight for observation, but you can pick him up tomorrow afternoon."

Faith didn't remember agreeing to this, but what else could she do? She released a heavy breath. She'd been overruled. "We'll be here."

She wasn't doing this on her own. Mrs. Watson seemed anxious to volunteer, so she would be the one to care for him. Faith had no intention of utilizing her medical background—ever. How could she? The memories were too haunting.

Chapter Three

The following afternoon at the inn, Joshua burrowed his throbbing head back into a mound of oversize down pillows. "This really isn't necessary. I'll be fine. Besides, the doctor said it was only a mild concussion. He did release me, you know?"

"It's not 'only.' A concussion of any degree shouldn't be ignored."

He eyed Faith, wondering how she'd ended up with the short straw. Judging from her stiff posture and stony expression, playing babysitter wasn't something she wanted any part of. "So how did you get stuck with me?" He'd rather have stayed at the hospital than be cared for by the woman whose life he was going to turn upside down.

"You were fortunate. Head injuries aren't something to take lightly. Like it or not, we're stuck with each other for the next forty-eight hours. Mrs. Watson is supposed to help, but she's had some sort of emergency in the kitchen." She turned toward the plantation shutters, closing both.

"I just took a little tumble." He knew God had been watching over him yesterday, and for that he was thankful. He'd skied long enough to know the risks involved. Years ago, a good friend from college was left paralyzed following a skiing accident. "This all seems like a little too much, don't you think?"

"Actually...no." She picked up a pitcher of water sitting on the dresser and poured him half a glass. "You need to let me know if you develop a headache or if you experience any dizziness or blurred vision." Faith placed the water on the nightstand.

"How did you become such an expert on concussions? Is it part of some training you had to take to work here?"

She fidgeted with the gold chain around her neck. "Something like that."

Boy, he'd been around some tight-lipped people before, but hers were cemented shut. It was obvious his questions were making her uncomfortable, but why? "Can you please hand me my laptop? It's over there on the desk."

Faith firmly planted her hands on her hips.

"You can't use your computer for the next two days."

This was outrageous. He wasn't going to put his life on hold because of a slight bump on the head. He had too much work to do to get ready for the auction. "Please bring it to me."

Her feet appeared glued to the floor.

He peeled back the tan-and-black flannel blanket and placed his feet on the gleaming hardwood floor. "Fine—I'll get it myself."

Her face turned cherry red. "You most certainly will not! Get back in the bed." She lunged toward him. "You don't seem to understand the precautions that must be taken following a head injury. You're my responsibility and I'm telling you, complete bed rest is a must. That means no computers, television or reading."

Releasing a heavy sigh, he flopped back against the pillows and covered himself with the blanket. "Can I at least have my phone?"

"No electronics of any kind. Do you understand?"

He didn't understand. A thought surged into his mind: Could she know the real reason why he was here? Was that why she was keeping such a close eye on him and not even allowing him access to his business files? There was no point in hiding the reason he was in Whispering Slopes. She'd find out sooner or later anyway. "Please, let me have my laptop. I have pressing business to address."

She shook her head. "I'm sorry. Nothing is so important to jeopardize your well-being. Please don't make me remove your devices from the room."

Joshua shot her a look. "Look—I may as well be up-front with you. I'm here for the auction." He gripped the blanket, prepared for her reaction.

Silence filled the room. For a second, he wished he hadn't removed the batteries from the clock. The ticking would be better than the sound of her angry breaths.

Faith fiddled with the guest towels before she finally spoke. "If that's the only reason you've come, you're wasting your time. There's not going to be an auction."

Obviously, the woman was in denial. And why wouldn't she be? She'd lose her home and possibly her job. Maybe he could hire her—but really, why would she want to work for him? "What makes you say that?"

She rolled her shoulders back. "I plan to contact the owner before the auction. I'll make him an offer, so an auction won't be necessary."

"And you have that kind of—" He bit his tongue, realizing he'd overstepped his bounds, but it was too late.

Her face grimaced. "Not right at the moment, but I'll get it. This property is way too important to me to let it go. I'll explain it to the owners. They'll understand."

If she only knew whom she was up against, she'd realize she was fighting a losing battle. His father couldn't care less about her family. He certainly didn't care about his own. "I wouldn't count on it."

Faith approached his bed and crossed her arms. "How would you know?"

"The so-called sympathetic owner happens to be my father. I'll give you a heads-up... he's the least understanding person you'll ever meet." He knew the man well enough to know money always came first. RC Carlson wouldn't give a hoot if this place was important to her. If he had any heart at all, his own son wouldn't be going behind his back to try and purchase the inn.

She stared at the ground and then tilted her head up. "Your father owns this property?"

Giggles outside the door and a light knock brought an abrupt end to their discussion.

"Faith, it's Joy. Are you in there?"

"It's my sister. She has Bella with her today."

He sat up a little more, curious to meet Faith's twin. "By all means, we might as well have the entire family in on this conversation."

She shot him a glare before opening the door.

"Mr. Joshua!" Bella tore into the room and bounded onto the bed. "Are you okay?" She nuzzled her head into his shoulder and his heart melted.

"I'm just fine…well, I would be if your mother ever lets me out of this bed, or at least allows me to use my laptop. She seems to be the expert on concussions."

Bella pulled away. "She was almost a doctor."

His eyes narrowed as he turned to Faith. "Almost a doctor?"

She strolled toward her daughter and hoisted her off the bed. "Bella, go downstairs and see if Mrs. Watson needs any help in the kitchen. We'll be down in a couple of minutes—run along, now."

At the door, the child turned. "I hope you're better in time for the snowman-making contest, Mr. Joshua. You can be on our team." She skipped out the door, whistling a melody.

Faith's sister approached his bedside. "Hello, I'm Joy." She extended her slender hand and smiled.

Both women had caramel hair and fair coloring, but their chestnut eyes were different. Faith had a far-off sadness in her eyes; the light had been extinguished. Maybe it had to do with

Bella not having a father around, but perhaps that had been by choice.

He shook Joy's hand. "I'd stand up, but she might chain me to the bed." He tipped his head in Faith's direction. "It's a pleasure to meet you, Joy." He smiled. "All joking aside, I am thankful for your sister's help when I fell. Being stuck on top of a mountain overnight isn't on my bucket list."

Her smile was warm, unlike her sister's.

"It sounds as though she returned the favor," she stated.

"What do you mean?" Faith interjected as she walked closer toward the bed.

"Well, you were there to help Joshua yesterday on the slopes and he helped you find Bella the other evening." Joy smiled at Joshua. "According to my niece, you came out from nowhere, like a superhero. That's what she called you."

His face heated. "I don't know about that—anyone would have done the same."

"Faith tells me you plan to stay for several weeks. You must work in a business that allows you the luxury of working anywhere."

"Actually, Joshua is here to bid on the inn. Isn't that right?" Faith's eyes practically seared his skin.

He'd gone from superhero to villain in a matter of seconds. "Ah...yes, it is."

"He was just telling me RC Carlson—you know, the man I write my rent check to—is his father. Small world, isn't it?"

Beads of sweat peppered his forehead. "Listen, I'm not really up to discussing this right now." His head pounded. Perhaps there was more to this concussion thing than he realized.

She reached for Joy's arm. "Let's go. He needs his rest."

Faith turned before exiting. "I'll have Mrs. Watson bring up your dinner."

His stomach churned. "No, thank you. I think I'll hold out until breakfast. I really just want to sleep."

"Okay, but dial 99 if you need anything. The call will forward to my house."

And with that, she pulled the door shut.

Joshua released a heavy breath. He'd thought being up-front with Faith would relieve some of his guilt, but unfortunately, it hadn't happened. The sweet little girl who'd showed so much concern could lose her home, thanks to him. But what else could he do? He had to move forward to honor his mother's memory. She'd always been there for him—he needed to be there for her.

* * *

"Mommy, can I wear my white dress to church today?"

With her hands wrapped around a steaming cup of coffee, Faith sat at the kitchen table and gazed out the window. The black-capped chickadees were busy devouring the birdseeds she'd put out yesterday. "No, sweetie, that's a summer dress."

"I can wear my heavy coat—please."

Opposite the feeder, the thermometer read twenty degrees. "It's below freezing outside. Put on the pretty long-sleeved black-and-white dress." She took a slow and easy sip. Caffeine—exactly what she needed this morning. She thought back about the past couple of days. She hadn't realized until last night, as she tossed and turned in bed, how emotionally draining it had been being back in a hospital, especially the ER. To make matters worse, now she'd been forced to care for a man whose business plan would make her homeless and unemployed. Where would she and Bella go? Whispering Slopes was the only home they'd known.

Patent leather shoes tapped along the hardwood floor. "Mommy, will Mr. Joshua be okay?"

She turned toward the doorway and her heart

squeezed. Bella had a way of melting her worries. Wearing Faith's favorite dress, her daughter looked like a princess. "I think he'll be fine. Mrs. Watson is keeping a close eye on him today. He just needs rest." She headed toward the pantry and pulled out a box of cereal, trying to ignore the concerns she had about Bella's growing attachment to Joshua.

"Why aren't we having pancakes?" Bella's shoulders drooped as she took a seat at the table.

Sunday morning pancakes were a tradition for a couple of years; they'd been Bella's father's favorite. After he died, she'd continued the tradition with her daughter. With her mind on the auction and playing nurse, she'd completely forgotten. "I'm sorry, there's not enough time for pancakes this morning." She poured the chocolate puffs into Bella's favorite cereal bowl and bit her lip. "What if we have them for dinner instead?"

Bella's chair squeaked as she bobbled up and down. "That's even better."

"It is?" Faith poured the milk and placed the bowl in front of Bella.

"Because pancakes are for breakfast—we're breaking the rules." She giggled and scooped a spoon of puffs into her mouth.

Faith ran her hand through her daughter's

curls. "You're a goof—now eat. Mrs. Underwood will be here any minute to take you to Sunday school."

Bella took a sip of her orange juice. "Why aren't you taking me?"

She didn't want her daughter to know anything about the auction until she had all the facts. Faith strolled to the coffeepot and poured another cup. "Aunt Joy is coming over this morning. I have to talk with her about something."

Bella swallowed her last bite. "About what?" She lifted the bowl and started to drink the now-chocolate milk.

Faith reached for her hand. "Use your manners, please." She took the dish, placed it into the stainless-steel sink and turned on the faucet. "If you want chocolate milk, you'll drink it from a glass, not a bowl. Now hurry along and brush your teeth."

"But I want to stay and listen."

Faith walked toward her daughter with her arms crossed. "Bella."

Bella gulped down the last of her juice and zipped toward her bedroom.

Gravel crunched outside. Faith glanced out the window and spied Mrs. Underwood's minivan cruising up the driveway. The horn tooted. Faith opened the front door, just off from the kitchen. She waved as a blast of January air smacked her in the face. "She'll be right out." Shutting out the cold, she shuffled into the laundry room and grabbed her sweater. "Bella, your ride is here," she yelled down the hallway.

"Coming." The girl tore into the laundry room and snatched her coat.

"Aunt Joy and I will see you after Sunday school." Faith stooped down and kissed her cheek.

"Love you, Mommy." She hopped down the porch steps and rushed to the van.

Fifteen minutes later, dressed in a tan pantsuit with a long-sleeved chocolate turtleneck underneath, Faith topped off her coffee and placed it into the microwave for one minute. Her heart squeezed as she recalled how special Sunday morning coffee used to be before Chris died. As though they were the only people in the world, they'd share their hopes and desires during those precious predawn hours. Their first dream had come to fruition with the birth of their daughter. The second had died in the fire, along with Chris.

The microwave beeped. Faith removed the steaming mug as the sound of a car door slamming signaled her twin's arrival. Her heart raced, anxious to get Joy's thoughts on the auction.

A chilly draft consumed the room as Joy

made her entrance into the foyer and sauntered into the kitchen. "So what's so urgent, sis? The message you left at three o'clock this morning sounded a little cryptic." She reached for a coffee mug and poured herself a cup before stripping off her coat and flinging it across the back of the kitchen table chair. "What on earth were you doing up so early?"

"Trying to quiet my racing mind—I need to talk to you about something."

Joy studied her twin. "What's wrong? Is Bella okay?"

"Yes, she's fine. It's about the inn going up for auction." Saying it out loud made it even more real.

Joy's brow crinkled as she slumped into the chair. "What's the big deal? Businesses go under new management all of the time and nothing changes. You and Bella won't be forced to move, and you'll be able to keep your job—after all, you're the reason the place is so successful."

Their voices fell silent as a cardinal chirped outside the window.

Despite her worries, she smiled. "I never told you, but Chris and I talked about purchasing an inn one day. At first, I thought it was silly, but Chris really wanted it. In time, I warmed up to the idea and actually became as excited as he'd been. We spent hours huddled around the kitchen table making plans. I have two notebooks packed with our ideas, sketches, costs—everything." Faith shivered. "If only we'd put our dream into action sooner, he'd be alive."

"Come on, don't go down the road of blaming yourself. Chris loved his job."

True—but she'd pushed him into a field he'd never considered, all because she needed security. What kind of security did she have now? Sure, there was a life insurance for Bella's college tuition, but she'd lost her best friend, Bella had lost her daddy, and sadly, Chris had never fulfilled his dream. "I'm thinking about bidding on the Black Bear..." Her voice trembled.

Joy's mouth dropped open. "Are you serious?"

Tears escaped Faith's eyes. "I forced Chris into a job he never wanted. He would have been content to work along with his father, building furniture for the family business."

"You know that wasn't Chris."

Maybe it wasn't, but at least he'd still be alive. She'd have a husband, and her daughter, a father. "There wasn't any security in that position. His father always struggled to make ends meet and he couldn't afford to send any of their children to college." Faith wiped her eyes. "I didn't want that for our future children." She swallowed hard to force down the lump lodged in her throat. "Or for me. I was selfish and greedy."

"Wanting security for your family isn't being greedy, Faith."

A sense of excitement missing for years returned, as adrenaline coursed through her body. Maybe the auction wasn't meant to be bad news. Perhaps it was an opportunity for Chris's dream and hers to live on—for her to provide security for her daughter. She sprung from her chair. "I'll be right back," she yelled over her shoulder as she took off down the hall. Her feet skidded on the hardwood floor.

Inside her bedroom, she dropped to her knees and yanked open the lid to the pine chest sitting at the foot of her bed. Underneath Bella's baby blanket—their dream. She snatched the two spiral notebooks and clutched them close to her heart. Tears moistened her eyelashes as she recalled the day she'd packed them away—the day she buried her husband. Tossing the blanket inside the chest, she closed the lid. On her way back to the kitchen, she grabbed a tissue from the box on her dresser. *I'm going to do this, sweetheart—for us.* She blotted her eyes and bolted out of the bedroom, excited to share their plan with her sister.

"What's come over you? You're glowing like

the top of Cape Hatteras Lighthouse," Joy said as she picked up one of the spiral notebooks Faith had placed in front of her. "Is this it?"

Faith took her seat. "And this." She slid the second notebook in front of her twin. "This is three years of dreaming and planning, right up until the day before he died. I want to do this, Joy. I've never wanted anything so bad in my life."

Joy leaned back into her chair, flipping through page after page of scribbled notes. She carefully closed the book. "Well, remember what grandmother always said. 'If you've got a dream, track it like a bloodhound.' I say go for it, sis."

Tears streamed down her cheeks. "Really? You're behind me on this?"

Joy laughed. "Does it really matter? You've got your mind set—I know you."

"Of course it does. Your opinion means a lot to me." She fingered her necklace. "As a kid, I always wanted your approval." She smiled and reached for Joy's hand. "I guess nothing has really changed."

"A lot has. You've been through so much in the past four years, losing Chris and raising Bella on your own. I'm so proud to call you my sister. You're the strongest person I know, Faith." Joy wiped away a tear and straightened her shoulders. "I think God has orchestrated this auction just for you."

Her, strong? The weeks following Chris's death, she'd been about as strong as a newly fledged hummingbird. "I couldn't have survived those first couple of years without you, sis." Faith leaned back in her chair and folded her arms. "As for God, I'm not so sure about Him being behind this." She watched her sister's reaction. "You know we're not exactly on speaking terms."

"That doesn't matter. He still loves you and wants the best for you. He'll work everything out for good, if you open your heart to Him."

The hum of the refrigerator hung in the air.

Joy squirmed in her chair and leaned forward. "About yesterday, let me make sure I've got this straight," she said with a grin. "That gorgeous man, Joshua, is your boss's son and your landlord, too…very interesting."

She couldn't argue the facts. He was handsome. "I thought there was something up with him." Faith sat forward and placed her elbows on the table. "What I don't understand is why Joshua's father doesn't just give him the property."

"Maybe he doesn't know his son's interested."

Faith drummed her fingers along her lips. "I suppose, but why keep it a secret?"

"People keep secrets for different reasons. Why didn't you ever tell me you've dreamed of owning an inn?"

Her stomach sank. "After Chris died, I didn't see any reason to harp on a dream that was over."

A smile curled across Joy's lips. "So…how does it feel to bring it back to life?"

"Exhilarating. Scary." Could she do this? She let her gaze drift toward the window and the snow-covered mountains. This land had always been her home. She couldn't lose it now. "I think I'll have to take out a loan."

"What about the insurance—"

"No!" Faith shook her head. She refused to touch the life insurance money. One thing she knew for sure—life could change in a heartbeat and you must be prepared. That money was the only way she could provide a secure future for her daughter.

"I can help you." Joy squeezed her sister's hand. "You know I've got a good pension through the school's retirement plan. I could borrow from my 401(k)."

Faith shook her head. "No way. It's your security. I won't have you tapping into those funds."

"But I believe in your dream. If anyone can make this happen, it's you…don't ever forget it."

Faith didn't know what she'd do without her sister. "I won't...thanks."

"Maybe you could talk to Joshua? Let him know the inn was your childhood home after Mom and Dad were killed, and we went to live with Grandma and Grandpa."

"He already knows, but it doesn't matter to him. He wants it as much as I do."

Joy's brow arched. "And you know that after only a couple days?"

She shrugged her shoulders. "If only we'd been here, instead of away at college, maybe we could have helped Grandma and Grandpa financially and prevented RC Carlson from purchasing their property? It would have been nice to have kept their house in the family."

"Well, as determined as you are, I think you'll get what you want."

Faith only hoped she could stay strong and fight for the property. Being back in the hospital and then having to use her medical skills to care for Joshua had sapped her strength. Who was she kidding? She was weak. Anyone who dropped out of medical school because they have panic attacks—at a hospital of all places—was pathetic.

But she was about to show her strength.

Chapter Four

Joshua squirmed in the front seat of Faith's SUV. It smelled like lavender, his mother's favorite fragrance. He buckled his seat belt, thankful Tuesday morning had finally arrived. Cute as she might be, he couldn't wait to be released from Faith's care. She'd been like a hawk, watching over every move. Now it was time to get back to the business of keeping the inn for his mother. "I thought Mrs. Watson was driving me to my doctor's appointment."

Faith yanked down the visor as the morning sun streamed through the windshield. "She had to stay and help Michael. He's preparing a special meal for tonight."

"I know this is the last thing you want to be doing—so thanks."

"It's not a problem."

They traveled in silence for the remainder

of the fifteen-minute drive. Faith hit the turn signal when they reached the parking lot of the hospital.

Once inside, Joshua took a seat in the waiting room. Faith made him nervous as she paced the floor. "Why don't you have a seat?" Her heels pecked against the tile. When he was married to Jessica, her stiletto shoes had always annoyed him. But now, even though she'd broken the vows they'd made before God over love for another man and money, he missed the sound.

It made him think about Jessica. Had she ever really loved him? He certainly had loved her. And he had to admit that a tiny part of him couldn't wait for her to get wind of his new business venture.

"The receptionist said the doctor was behind schedule because of a multicar accident." He patted his hand on the empty brown vinyl chair next to his, but Faith turned and walked toward the vending machine.

Joshua pulled his phone from his back pocket. Ten new messages. According to the call log, four of those calls had been from his attorney, Melissa. He wondered if she had any updated news about the auction. He'd call her once he was back at the inn and away from Faith's watchful eyes.

A few minutes later, Faith strolled toward him with a cup of coffee in each hand and sank into a chair beside him. "I'd thought you'd like some."

"Thank you." Surprised by her gesture, he reached for the cup and noticed her hand quivered. "Are you okay?"

"Of course I am…why wouldn't I be?"

"You just seem a little tense." Was she afraid the doctor wouldn't release him and she'd be stuck with him even longer? "I feel fine, so don't worry that I won't get cleared today. I don't have the slightest headache and I'm not dizzy. By the time we leave here, you'll be able to hang up your nurse's cap." He sipped his beverage. Not bad for hospital coffee.

"The thought never crossed my mind."

When the overhead intercom paged a Dr. James, Faith's body jerked and her shoulders tightened.

"Oh, yeah, you're as calm as a buoy in a tidal wave."

A few moments later, two paramedics burst through the doors of the ER. The gurney whizzed by carrying what appeared to be a burn victim. A young woman drowning in tears ran alongside, trying to keep up.

Faith's cup dropped to the tile floor, splattering its contents in all directions. Her face turned white as a snowdrop flower. Her eyes remained glued on the gurney as it was rushed down the hall.

He cautiously reached for her hand in an attempt to calm her violent shakes. "Faith...what is it? Are you sick?"

Her gaze stayed fixated on the doors, long after they were closed.

"Please, let me help you."

"You can't—no one can." She slid back into her chair.

"Let me at least try," he pleaded.

Faith's eyelids closed and tears rolled down her cheeks. "My husband, Chris—" She gulped in some air as she struggled for her words. "He was a firefighter."

Was. His stomach turned over at the word. This was why her eyes reflected pools of sadness.

"Four years ago, he was severely burned in a fire here in Whispering Slopes when the Bluefield Mill burned to the ground. We lost four brave men when the ceiling collapsed. Chris was one of those four."

He had difficulty swallowing against the hard knot at the back of his throat. "I'm so sorry, Faith."

"For a week, I paced the floors of this horrible place, after the other three men had already passed away. I cried out to God to let my husband regain consciousness. I needed to apologize to him." She leaned forward and rested her elbows on her knees, covering her face. "He died on the eighth day. God didn't listen to my prayers." She rubbed her eyes with the back of her hand and sucked in quick, shaky breaths. "I was never able to tell him how wrong I was."

He'd assumed Faith was divorced or maybe had chosen not to marry Bella's father. He'd never imagined a tragedy like this. Guilt washed over him. Because of his accident, she'd been forced to come back to this hospital and relive those painful memories.

Joshua stood and reached out his hand to help her out of the chair. He couldn't stand to see her in pain. "We need to get you out of here."

She stayed firm in her seat, her back now ramrod straight. "No, you need to see the doctor. I'll be fine."

"I can do this alone. You should go outside and wait in the car. I think a little fresh mountain air would do you some good."

A short brunette dressed in polka-dot scrubs approached. "Mr. Carlson?" The thick accent identified her as a local.

Joshua stood. "Yes, that's me."

"The doctor will see you now." She turned on her heel like a military soldier. "Follow me, please."

He extended his hand to Faith and she accepted. "You don't have to do this, you know."

For the first time since she'd picked him up for his appointment, she gave a hint of a smile. It was nice.

"I want to—really, I do." She raked her hand through her loose curls. "Somehow, I need to break the chains of this place. I can't keep running away."

As they followed the nurse down the hall, Faith's words replayed in his head about the fire. *I needed to apologize.* He couldn't help but wonder what she'd done that she had to ask for her dying husband's forgiveness.

Wednesday afternoon, Joshua checked his calendar as he sat at the desk in his room. He had a telephone conference call scheduled in an hour with Melissa and his financial advisor, Joe. He'd earned a lucrative salary working for his father over the years and had plenty of money squirreled away in his money market account, but he wanted to make sure he had enough available funds to outbid anyone who tried to stand in his way. The last thing he wanted to do was to tap into the trust account his father had set up for him. This was something he had to do on his own.

"Plato, come back here!"

The sound of tiny feet running down the hall echoed outside his door. Moments later, a soft knock sounded.

"Come in, Bella."

Tentatively, she crossed the threshold, holding Plato tight in her arms. A sweet smile tugged on her pouty pink lips. "How did you know it was me?"

"You're the only person I know with a dog named Plato."

She giggled. "He wanted to come and visit you." She flopped down in the leather chair. "Are you feeling better?"

"I'm good as new—thank you."

Bella bounced up and down in her seat. "Goody! So you can come to the snowman-making contest. It's not this Saturday, but next."

When she'd first mentioned it the other day, he wasn't so sure about going. But the more he'd thought about it, the more he figured it might make for great public relations. After all, it could be a good opportunity for him to get to know the townspeople. "Sure, I'd love to go. So tell me, where is your mother today?" He hadn't seen her when he went down for both breakfast and lunch. He couldn't really blame her for trying to avoid him.

"She had appointments today. Aunt Joy brought me home from school. She's downstairs."

Appointments? Was she taking care of business and getting ready for the auction, too?

"How was school today?"

"It was good. Brian Woody got in trouble for eating glue."

Joshua laughed out loud. This little girl was adorable and such a joy to have around. "I can't imagine it tasted very good."

She shook her head. "Do you have kids, Mr. Joshua?"

"No, I don't."

"You'd make a good daddy."

His heart tightened. "What a nice thing to say." Maybe if he made it a point to be the complete opposite of his own father.

"I don't have a daddy." She released a long sigh. "I did, but he died. I don't even know what he looked like."

No wonder she'd latched on to him so quickly. "I'm so sorry, Bella. Don't you have pictures of him?"

Her ponytails swung side to side. "No, Mommy has them all locked away."

She had to have been mistaken. What possible reason could Faith have for denying this child all she had left of her father?

"Bella!" The door that had been left ajar flew wide open. "What are you doing in here bothering Mr. Joshua?" Faith's face was fire-engine red.

Bella jumped from the chair, squeezing Plato tight. "I just wanted to say hi."

"You shouldn't be bothering our guests." Faith pointed toward the door. "Please go downstairs and wait for me in the kitchen."

Bella tipped her chin toward the ground and exited the room.

He locked his eyes on Faith. "Don't you think you were a little hard on her? I was actually enjoying her company."

"I'd appreciate it if you didn't question how I punish my daughter. She had no right to come up here and disturb you."

This wasn't just about Bella paying him a visit. Right now, she could spit nails. There was something else going on. But he knew it was best to drop it. "You're right. I'm sorry."

Faith rubbed her hand across her forehead and blew out a heavy breath. "No, I'm the one who should apologize. I shouldn't have overreacted, but I don't like her bothering the guests."

"Trust me, your child could never be a bother to me. She's an absolute delight to have around." *As for her mother—not so much.* Her stiff posture spoke loud and clear as she left the room. Moments later, his thoughts drifted back to Bella. Had she really never seen photos of her own father? How could Faith be so insensitive to her daughter's needs when it was so obvious how much she loved her?

Late Saturday afternoon, the winter sun was sinking fast as Faith scurried through the grocery store with Bella. She'd planned on making her daughter's favorite dinner, spaghetti with giant meatballs. When she discovered she didn't have any tomatoes left for the homemade sauce, they'd piled into the car for a quick trip to the market.

"Can we get these, Mommy?" Bella pointed to a box of chocolate-covered donuts with chopped walnuts sprinkled on the top.

"No, not today." Faith announced as she grabbed a wheat baguette and placed it into her basket. "Hurry along. I want to get home before dark." Although she'd lived here all her life, she still didn't like to drive the curvy mountain roads after dark. Rounding the corner, she plowed straight into a wall of solid muscle, sending her groceries flying. The tomatoes rolled like rubber balls across the tiled floor. "Excuse—"

"Faith."

Since her outburst about Bella's visit to his room, she'd done a good job of avoiding the inn's longest-staying guest. "Joshua. I'm sorry. I wasn't paying attention." She bit down on her lower lip and kneeled to retrieve her items.

"Hi, Mr. Joshua!" Bella raced to his side, her neon-pink tennis shoes bouncing off the ground.

"Hello, Bella." Dressed in jeans and a black leather jacket, he headed down the aisle. "Let me grab those runaway tomatoes for you." The smell of sweet peppermint lingered in the air.

"I'll help." Bella took off behind him.

Faith scooped the contents back inside the basket. She'd never had good timing.

Joshua sauntered toward her with a tomato in each hand. "I'm not so sure about this one."

He handed her the now mushy vegetable.

She inspected it closely and nodded. "Yeah, I better go swap this one out. Come along, Bella." She turned on her heel and headed toward the produce section.

"See you at home," Bella shouted over her shoulder as Joshua remained standing in the middle of the aisle.

Outside in the parking lot, the sun was preparing to rest in the western sky. Glints of orange shimmered over the mountains. Faith paused to take in the beauty. This was why she'd always call Whispering Slopes home.

"Mommy, the tire looks like a pancake." Bella announced as Faith struggled to hold the bag of groceries while her right hand fumbled deep inside her purse for her car keys.

She approached her vehicle and her shoulders slumped when she realized Bella was right. It had only been three weeks since she'd replaced all four tires, so at least they were still under warranty. But it didn't solve her problem of being stranded in the supermarket parking lot right now, with no idea how to put on a spare. Chris had always tried to teach her, but she wasn't interested. Besides, she knew that he'd always be a phone call away. Her heart squeezed.

"Can we drive with it like that, Mommy?"

"Unfortunately, we can't. I'll have to call road service." Knowing sometimes they could take a while to arrive, she pulled her phone from her purse and tapped the screen.

"Look, here comes Mr. Joshua. He can help us." Bella ran toward the front of the store.

"Watch for cars!" she yelled as she slipped her phone back inside her bag. She watched as Bella approached him. Bella's arms flailed in all directions as she obviously overdramatized the situation, like she often did. He took her hand and led her across the parking lot.

She swallowed the knot forming in the back of her throat as Joshua walked toward the car. It should have been Chris holding his daughter's hand and coming to her rescue, not the man who wanted to take away everything that mattered most to her.

"Bella wasn't kidding. The tire sure is a pancake." He set his two bags of groceries on the blacktop and took off his leather jacket. "Can you pop the trunk? I'll grab the spare and have you on your way in no time."

For a moment, she hesitated. Glancing up at the inky sky, she realized having Joshua take care of her problem would at least get her and Bella on the road sooner. She opened the back door and placed her groceries on the floor before pressing the button to unlatch the trunk. When her cell phone chirped, she removed it from her purse and scanned the screen. "It's Mrs. Watson. I'm sorry, I'll need to take this. She wouldn't call me if there wasn't a problem." She stepped aside so Joshua could get to work.

"Of course," he said, reaching inside to retrieve the spare.

Faith turned her attention to the call. "Mrs. Watson—what's up?"

The sounds of sirens and men yelling echoed

through the phone. "Faith, you need to get to the inn." The elderly woman coughed. "Now!"

The phone shook against her ear. Mrs. Watson's voice was drenched in panic. "What is it? What's wrong?" Faith asked.

She stared at her phone in disbelief after the line went dead. "The inn. It's on fire!"

Chapter Five

"Mommy, are we going to lose our house?" Bella's question packed a punch, causing his gut to twist. If they lost their home, it wouldn't be from the fire.

Inside his car, Faith shot Joshua a look as though she'd read his mind. They both wanted the inn, but neither was likely to budge.

"No, sweetie. I'm sure it will be fine. The fire is at the inn, but hopefully it won't be so bad."

"But Plato is home alone." Bella's voice quivered.

Joshua white-knuckled the steering wheel of his Mercedes. After the call from Mrs. Watson, they'd locked up her car and raced to his. *Please, Lord, let their house be safe. And let the inn be spared.*

He glanced into his rearview mirror as the

sound of sirens cried out in the darkness. "I've got to pull over, since there's another fire truck coming up behind us."

"I'm scared, Mommy." Bella covered her ears while Joshua veered off on a side road. "What if the fire's like the one Daddy was in? What will happen to Plato?" she wailed.

Minutes later, he was back on the road, apprehensive about what they'd find when they reached the inn.

"Can't you go any faster?" Faith pleaded.

He glanced at the speedometer. He was already over the speed limit. "I'm not as familiar with the twists and turns of these roads—safety first." He squeezed the wheel tighter as his vehicle hugged the curves.

Finally, they pulled into the parking lot of the inn. Faith's eyes grew wide as they assessed the damage. A billowing, smoky haze blanketed the Black Bear. Orange flames shot from the kitchen window.

She gasped and flung her hand over her mouth. "My inn!" Tears filled her eyes.

My inn. His muscles tensed at her words. She had no right to stake a claim on something belonging to his mother.

"Plato! We have to save him!" Bella called out, peering from the back seat.

Faith sprung from the car. "They must have called stations from the surrounding counties." Joshua got out, as well, and Bella scrambled out quickly.

Before Joshua could shut the car door, Bella wrapped her arms around his waist and coughed. "I'm scared, Mr. Joshua." She sniffed. "We have to find Plato."

With one swoop, he scooped the child into his arms. "Don't worry. I'll find him, sweetheart."

Taking long strides, Joshua rushed toward the entrance as Faith followed. "How bad is it?" he asked a firefighter who was walking out the front door.

Faith pushed her way past Joshua, confronting the man. "I'm the manager. Did everyone make it out safe?"

"The guests were all evacuated, but the ambulance just transported your chef to the hospital."

"Oh, no, not Michael! What—how…will he be okay?"

Joshua wondered if Faith and Michael had more than an employee-boss relationship. They seemed more like family. In fact, all of the employees at the inn appeared to be close.

"He suffered some severe burns. I'm not sure how bad."

"I can drive you to the hospital, if you'd like," Joshua said with hopes of calming her.

She ran both hands through her hair. "Yes, I want to see him, but I need to know how much damage we're dealing with. Can you tell me?" She pulled her eyes off the inn and turned to the firefighter.

"A few of the crew are still working. I do know the fire was contained to the kitchen, but it's extensive."

Faith gasped, but held her tongue.

Joshua cleared his throat and addressed the firefighter. "Do you know what caused the fire?"

"It appears there was unattended food left on the stove."

Faith shook her head. "That sure doesn't sound like Michael."

"What about Plato?" Bella cried out as she wiggled free from Joshua's arms. "He likes the big pillow in the kitchen."

Joshua turned toward the side of the inn and spotted Mrs. Watson with Plato snuggled in her arms. "He's right over there." As soon as Joshua pointed, Bella shot across the frosty ground.

"Bella!" Faith shouted and took off running after her daughter.

Mrs. Watson looked in their direction. "Faith, I'm so glad you're here—it was awful…poor Michael."

Bella snatched Plato into her arms. "Thank You, God, for protecting Plato." She smothered the white ball of fur with kisses.

"Do you know what happened, Mrs. Watson?" Faith asked while taking in deep and steady breaths.

Mrs. Watson's posture stooped. "It's my fault. The Wright family showed up early and a light bulb in their bathroom had burned out. My husband had gone into town. You know me and my fear of ladders. I asked Michael to help me. Oh, Faith, I could have burned the entire place to the ground."

Joshua placed his hand on the woman's slumped shoulders. "Relax, it was an accident."

She looked at Faith, tears streaming down her cheeks. "I'm so sorry. I know how much the inn means to you, and it's the only home you and Joy have ever known." Her voice quivered.

Joshua watched the two women embrace. *The only home she'd known.* But it was his mother's favorite place.

"No, no." Faith rubbed Mrs. Watson's back. "I should have stayed with you after some of the staff called in sick this morning. Please, stop blaming yourself—accidents happen." She gazed toward the inn, her eyes pooled with fear. "What about Michael? How bad is he?"

Mrs. Watson looked down at Bella, who was occupied with her puppy. She spoke in a whisper. "It's not good, dear." She reached for Faith's hand. "A grease fire got out of control. Once Michael was back inside the kitchen, he must have tried to extinguish it himself and his clothes caught fire. He ran out into the dining area and rolled around on the ground...oh, Faith, it was horrible."

Faith didn't need to hear any more of Mrs. Watson's play-by-play of the fire. Joshua turned to her. "Do you want to go with me? I'd like to speak with the firefighter in charge." When a couple of the fire trucks pulled out of the parking lot, he headed toward the remaining firefighters congregated by the front door. He wanted more details on the extent of the damage.

Faith nodded and kneeled down in front of Bella. "You and Plato stay here with Mrs. Watson. Whatever you do, don't wander off."

"Okay." The child responded and buried her cheek against her pup's muzzle.

Joshua eyed Faith as she stayed focused on the inn. Being around all of this emergency equipment and dealing with a fire had to be sparking horrifying memories of the night her husband was burned. "Hey—you okay?"

"I'm fine."

He wasn't convinced. How could she be?

"I need to know what we're dealing with," she whispered.

He agreed. Depending on the amount of damage, the auction could be delayed. And what if his father showed up at the inn to see what had happened? He could ruin everything.

"Faith! I've been looking for you."

A tall fireman with dirty blond hair carried his helmet as he approached Faith. He immediately wrapped his arms around her. "I'm so happy you weren't hurt."

"Danny, I'm glad you're here." Faith pulled away. "Joshua, this is Danny McMillian, from New Market. He used to work with my husband." Her voice was flat.

Joshua gripped the extended hand. "Thanks for getting things under control. How bad is it?"

"It could have been a lot worse. The inspector is on his way."

"What about the guests?" Faith turned to the group gathered close to Mrs. Watson.

"The smoke damage upstairs was minimal. They'll need to stay in a hotel tonight, but the restoration crew we use will do some thermal fogging and have them back into their rooms by tomorrow evening. But the kitchen appears to be a complete loss."

Faith squeezed her eyes tight; she then opened them and focused on Joshua. "How can we stay open without a kitchen?"

Good question and one he wasn't prepared to answer. He kicked his foot into the frozen ground and an idea sparked. But who was he kidding? She'd never go for it. Or would she?

The next morning, Faith sat at her kitchen table clutching her coffee cup. She'd barely slept. It was after midnight by the time the guests were settled into the hotel. Afterward, Joshua had driven her to the hospital to see Michael. She was grateful Joy had taken Bella to her house for an overnight stay. She needed this time to figure out how to feed everyone without a kitchen. Thankfully, Mr. Watson had agreed to meet with the restoration company while Mrs. Watson had offered to take the guests to Harrisonburg for a day trip, after church. They'd eat their meals out, before returning to the inn this evening. It bought her time for today to figure things out.

The gentle knock at her front door put her brainstorming on hold for now.

She gasped at the sight of her unexpected guest. He was looking tall, dark and incredibly handsome for seven o'clock in the morning. A shot of cold and damp air traveled deep inside her lungs, leaving her almost breathless. "Joshua, what are you doing here?"

She gripped the doorknob with her sweaty palm. Why did this man have to look more handsome each time she saw him? How was it possible? Yep. She definitely suffered from sleep deprivation.

Holding a brown bag, he extended his hand, wearing a crooked smile. "I thought you might be awake, too. I brought you some breakfast."

Although she was touched by his generosity, she could not help questioning his motives. "That wasn't necessary." The minute the words slipped through her lips, she knew she sounded ungrateful. "I'm sorry. It's very nice of you." She glanced down at her attire, embarrassed by her pink flamingo bathrobe. Desperate for a combing, she ran her hand through her hair. Her eyes darted around the cluttered kitchen as she stepped aside. "The place is kind of a mess, but you're welcome to come in." She should have taken the bag, thanked him and let him be on his way. Why did she invite him in? Now she'd have to eat breakfast with a man who seemed to have just stepped out of *GQ* while she probably looked like the lead character in a homemade horror film.

He entered the kitchen and the smell of peppermint followed. "I bought enough for two, so I had hoped you'd ask."

Faith scurried to the table. She gathered the piles of financial documentation she'd organized for her meeting at the bank and carried them to the nearby desk. She returned and grabbed two dirty glasses. "I apologize for the mess. Things have been a little hectic lately. I'm really not a slob—usually."

Joshua took off his leather jacket and hung it on the back of the chair. He opened the bag while Faith took two plates from the cupboard.

She lifted the pot. "Coffee?"

"Of course." He placed the bagels on one of the plates. "I got poppy seed and garlic, just in case you weren't a garlic gal."

Faith filled his mug. "Black, right?" The fact that she knew how he took his coffee caused her to shiver. It seemed wrong somehow. What seemed like yesterday, she'd only known how Chris drank his coffee.

"Perfect." He held the plate in front of her. "Pick one, you must be starving."

She snatched one and inhaled the zesty aroma. It was warm to the touch. "I've loved garlic since I was a kid."

He reached for the other. "Me, too." Joshua opened the brown bag and pulled out three containers of various flavors of cream cheese. "Pick again."

Faith sighed. "I'm not used to making so many decisions this early in the morning, or at least until I've had my second cup of coffee." She took a garlic-flavored packet. Her skin warmed when he reached for the same and their hands brushed.

"Wow, you do like it," he laughed and opened the pack of plain cream cheese. "Speaking of decisions—" He took a bite and chewed.

Faith pinched off a piece and popped it into her mouth…it was warm and delicious. "Yes?"

"You've got to decide how you're going to feed the guests." He took a sip of the strong brew. "Especially this one—I don't want to go hungry." He winked.

Joshua was right. Unless his father decided to shut the place down, it was her job to keep it open. "Yes, I do have some things to figure out."

He picked up the napkin from his lap and wiped his hands. "I have a proposal for you."

Her heart sped up. What could he possibly be proposing? "I'm listening."

"Well, your chef's in the hospital and he could be there for a few days."

True, but thankfully, after their visit last night, Faith had learned Mrs. Watson had a tendency to exaggerate. Michael had certainly been burned trying to extinguish the fire on his own, but the burns weren't nearly as bad as Mrs. Watson had made them out to be. "Mrs. Watson offered to cook, but I've eaten her food before." She crinkled her nose.

"No good?"

She nodded. "Her steak is as tough as shoe leather. And don't get me started on the asparagus. It's like slippery shoestrings."

Joshua released a deep belly laugh. "Well, then, you might like my suggestion after all."

She leaned back in her chair and crossed her arms. "I'm ready."

"It just so happens I'm a very good cook."

Faith's eyebrow shot up. "Really?"

"Don't get me wrong, I'm certainly not trying to brag, but I took some cooking classes a couple of years ago. I didn't want to at the time, but now I'm glad I did." A far-off look of sadness filled his eyes. "After my ex moved out of the house, I would have starved to death."

Faith had a feeling taking the classes had been his ex's idea. It was nice he'd done something he probably didn't want to do in order to make her happy. She couldn't help but wonder why the marriage didn't last. She'd give anything to be with Chris again. Pushing away those thoughts, she took another bite of her breakfast. "So, you can cook?"

He nodded. "I want you to think about it first and I hope you won't say no."

"Okay."

"What if I cook for the guests? I can plan all of the meals—I'll even grocery-shop. You won't have to worry about anything."

This was the last thing Faith expected to hear coming from Joshua's mouth. Why would he make such a generous offer? She was practically a stranger to him. "You want to take over Michael's responsibilities?"

"Why not? I'm capable of cooking most things, except I don't make fish."

"The smell?" Faith loved fish, but she couldn't stand to have her house smell fishy.

"Exactly. I love it, but I only eat it out at restaurants."

Faith laughed. "So you really want to do this? May I ask where you intend to make these five-star meals?"

Joshua pushed away from the table and walked to the gourmet six-burner stove. He turned to Faith and extended his arms. "Right here in your kitchen, of course."

She chomped hard on her lower lip and studied his face. There was no way she would allow it. With him as a guest, she could go out of her way to avoid him. But cooking here every day? It wasn't an option. "Why would you want to help me? You're a guest." A second later, it all made sense to her. "Oh, right, keep the guests happy so they'll return after you've taken ownership. Am I right?"

Joshua returned to his seat and placed his elbow on the table. He pressed his fist to his lips. He remained quiet, but only for a moment. "That's what you think? My offer is purely for selfish reasons?" He stood and picked up his plate. He placed it into the sink and turned. "I wanted to help you as a thank-you."

She crinkled her brow. "For what?"

"I felt bad about what happened at the hospital—when you took me to my appointment. If I'd known what you went through with your husband, I would have made other arrangements." He approached the table and grabbed his jacket. "No matter what you think of me, the offer stands."

Faith's stomach knotted. She'd hurt his feelings. Maybe his suggestion did come from a place of good intentions, but she had to stick to her plan. Keeping a safe distance from Joshua was the only way she'd have a chance at owning the inn. But she didn't like to cook and she certainly wasn't very good at it. What choice did she have?

"Okay, we'll start early tomorrow morning."

Chapter Six

Monday morning, with a light snow falling, Joshua headed out the door with his laptop in hand and ideas percolating. When he'd told Faith he'd be over early in the morning, he'd hoped 6:00 a.m. wasn't pushing it. The howling winds from the night before had settled to a light breeze as he strolled from his car toward her cottage. A forlorn whistle of a passing train in the distance sent a chill down his spine. As a child, he'd bury his head underneath his pillow to silence the lonesome sound. Even today, the memories the whistle triggered were ones he'd rather forget.

A light shining in the kitchen window caused his shoulders to relax a bit. Good. She was up and probably pacing the floor with a cup of coffee in hand, dreading his arrival. But the two had to put their differences aside and get past this hurdle that more than likely would delay the auction.

Not knowing if Bella was up for school, he lightly tapped his knuckle on the solid oak door.

"When you said early, you weren't kidding." Faith smiled as she moved aside to allow him to enter. Dressed in jeans and a crisp white shirt, and her hair pulled up in a tousled bun, she'd apparently been up for a while, too.

"I hope I'm not too early, but we've got a lot of planning to do. I've taken care of breakfast." His mind had been going nonstop since four o'clock this morning. "Mrs. Watson is going to run out and pick up bagels, fruit and yogurt for the guests. So we'll have to get going on lunch. I've got a ton of ideas for the week ahead."

"I'd offer you some coffee, but it appears you've already had plenty."

He walked toward the coffee maker, where Faith stood holding the pot. He reached for a mug on the counter and held it out in front of her. "One thing you'll learn about me, I can never have enough caffeine."

She filled his cup with the piping hot brew. "Well, at least there's one thing we can agree on."

They both settled down at the kitchen table and Joshua opened his laptop. "I've made up a calendar so we can record the meals for each day and pass it out to the guests."

"What a good idea." Faith opened up her spiral notebook. "I jotted down a few of Michael's specialties the guests seem to enjoy—nothing complicated." She slid the book in front of him.

"So what? You don't think I can cook anything more than beans and franks?"

Her face flushed. "No, that's not what I'm saying. I'm trying to make it as easy for you as possible. After all, you're doing this as a favor to me…at least, that's what you said yesterday."

Why was he being so defensive? She was only trying to help. "I'm sorry. I appreciate the list." He scanned the pages and nodded. "This is good. I know how to make most of these meals, except I don't cook chicken parmesan."

She leaned back in her chair and folded her arms. "But it's one of Michael's top dishes."

He took his red pen and scratched through the dish. "Sorry, but it's not an option." It had been his ex-wife's favorite meal. It was the first thing he'd ever cooked for her when they started dating. Now he wondered if she'd loved the dish more than him.

Faith watched him with a look of confusion. "Okay, then, how about fried chicken? Is it an option or should I nix anything in the poultry area?"

"Any other type of chicken is fine."

Faith's phone chimed. She frowned as she examined the screen.

"Is everything okay?"

"It's an email from your father's attorney about the kitchen renovations." She paused and continued to scan her device. "Apparently, it's going to be at least a month or maybe longer until everything is completed."

Joshua's shoulders slumped. Such a delay meant the auction probably wouldn't happen for at least a month.

Faith blew out an extended breath. "Oh, boy. You might want to reconsider your offer to cook. That's a long time."

It did seem like a lengthy amount of time for a kitchen. Could his father have possibly gotten wind of the fact his son planned to bid on the inn? He'd asked Melissa to keep this to herself. Surely, as his attorney, she wouldn't betray him? Could she be carrying a grudge after he'd up and married her best friend? Not that that had been the best decision he'd ever made.

"Well, it's a blessing we at least can use the dining room. I'm not sure you'd enjoy the guests eating three meals a day in your kitchen."

Her expression softened. "Can I ask you something?"

He rubbed the back of his neck. "Sure."

"Does your father know you're here to bid on the inn?"

"No, he doesn't—and I'd like to keep it that way."

Faith's eyebrows squished together. "I don't understand. If he knew you wanted the inn, wouldn't he just give it to you or at least let you purchase it directly from him?"

In a perfect family, it would probably be the scenario. But he'd known at a young age that his family was far from perfection. "It's a little more complicated." The argument leading up to his resignation flashed through his mind. He'd never seen his father so angry. But then again, Joshua had never felt rage like he had then. Sure, he could have handled it differently, but that day, his love for his mother had over-ridden his sense of reason.

Faith shook her head. "I'm sorry. I shouldn't meddle into family business."

He shrugged his shoulders. "Let's get back to the menu. I thought for lunch I could make some beef stew. How does that sound?"

"What's better on a snowy day? It sounds delicious."

"I'll make some corn bread to go along with it. My mother made the best I've ever tasted. I'll use her recipe." He tapped his fingers along the keyboard, entering the information into the calendar.

Faith smiled. "It sounds like you and your mother are close."

His fingers stopped typing as he locked eyes with hers. "She died recently." His attention turned back to the computer screen.

"I'm sorry. Had she been ill?"

Heaviness filled his heart. "She had cancer. It came on fast. She was gone in six months."

She shifted in her chair and fingered her gold chain.

He nodded. "To answer your question—yes, we were close." He swallowed the knot pressing against his throat. "She was the only person who ever believed in me."

Bella's voice echoing down the hall broke the silence.

Faith stood and pushed in her chair. "It's time for her to get ready for school."

He closed up the laptop and stood. "I'm going to head over to the hotel and finalize the menu for the week before I check out. Then I'll hit the grocery store." Taking note of the time on his phone, he grabbed his jacket. "I'll be back around ten fifteen to begin preparing lunch—if it's okay with you."

"That'll be fine." She strolled toward her purse sitting on the counter. "Let me give you the inn credit card for the groceries." Her eyes softened as she handed it to him. "I'm really sorry about your mother, Joshua."

"Thanks. I'll see you later."

Outside, the snow had tapered to flurries. Joshua stowed the computer in the trunk and rounded the car. Inside, he secured his seat belt and turned the ignition. When his phone chirped, he took a quick glance at the screen. He shifted in his seat. Why would his financial advisor be calling at this hour of the morning? "Hey, Joe, what's up?"

A brief delay on the line caused a moment of uneasiness. "You there?"

"Joshua, sorry, I couldn't hear you for a second."

Garbled voices carried through the phone. "Are you catching the subway already?" He turned off the car.

"Yeah, busy day today. Listen, I have some bad news."

Joshua's stomach quivered. The last time he'd heard those words was from his mother's doctor. "What is it?"

"I've been doing some number crunching. If you invest only the funds in your money market account for the auction, it might leave you a little thin in the wallet. I can't in good faith recommend you go forward with a financial decision so risky."

The last thing he wanted to do was to access any of his father's money to gain ownership of the inn, but there was no other way. "Go ahead and leave me enough in the account to keep me afloat for a year, and use the rest from my trust account."

"Well, that's the bad news, bud…uh, your father cut off your trust."

His heartbeat pounded in his eardrums. "What? Can he do that?"

"He's done it, so I guess so."

Before they said their goodbyes, Joe promised to call back in a day or two, giving him time to digest the news. Joshua blew out a heavy breath. He knew his father had been angry when he up and quit his job. They hadn't spoken since he quit, not even at the funeral, but cutting him off? Did he really hate his only son that much?

He sat in silence, shocked by the news. It was then he recalled one of his mother's favorite verses: *For I know the plans I have for you, declares the Lord, plans to prosper you and not to harm you, plans to give you hope and a future.* Smiling, he started the car and gazed out the window toward the sky. "Don't worry,

Mom, like you used to say, there's always hope when you put your trust into the Lord."

For dinner Thursday evening, Joshua had made the decision to take all the guests into town for pizza. He'd told Faith he thought she needed a break from him commandeering her kitchen, what seemed like every hour, since the fire.

The chili bubbled inside the slow cooker while the tomato and spinach salads chilled in the refrigerator. The aroma of the French baguette browning in the oven filled Faith's kitchen.

She'd decided she and Bella would forgo the trip into town with the others. Since the day she'd overheard her daughter telling Joshua about her father's photographs being locked away, Faith hadn't been able to get it out of her mind. She squeezed her eyes shut and tried to force the conversation from her brain. She couldn't imagine what he must think of her. Withholding photographs and not sharing any memories of Bella's father with her…who did such a thing? Why hadn't she ever thought of how this might affect her daughter? Her decision to pack away all of the pictures had been a selfish one—and one that had obviously backfired. Stuffing the photos away hadn't erased the pain; it only magnified the truth. Her husband had died because of her.

Faith inhaled a deep breath and released. "Dinner's ready, sweetie." In need of something to stop her hands from shaking, she hurried to the refrigerator and removed the salads. She unscrewed the lid to the Italian dressing and lightly poured it onto the salads. "Don't forget to wash your hands." After placing the greens on the table, she scooped two servings of chili into Bella's favorite bowls.

All smiles and whistling a tune, Bella skipped into the kitchen and plopped into her chair. Faith recalled when her daughter learned to skip at the age of three. Since then, whenever she entered a room, she was skipping.

"It smells good, Mommy. I love your chili."

Faith placed the meal on the table. No time like the present. She forced herself to relax and took a seat across from her daughter. "Do you know who else loved chili?"

"Who?"

She swallowed hard before speaking. "Your daddy—it was his favorite. He always thought the spicier the better."

"Just like me!"

Her husband had had a mouth made of cast iron. "Yes, exactly." Surprised by how good she felt, she wanted to share more. "Do you know what else he liked?"

"What?" Bella bounced up and down in her chair, anxious to hear the answer.

"He loved the miniature saltine crackers," she answered, scooping a handful from the box she had put there earlier and placing some into both bowls.

Bella's smile revealed the missing tooth that had fallen out last week. "Like me."

Faith blotted a tear with her napkin. "Exactly."

"What else—what else?" Bella spooned a heaping mouthful of meat and beans into her mouth.

Why had Faith waited so long? She wanted to bottle this feeling. Bella deserved to know what a wonderful man her father was and how much he loved her. "Your daddy loved the snow. Every year, after the first snow of the season, he'd make a snowman in the backyard. When it melted and another snow came, he'd do it all over again. He wanted a snowman guarding our house all winter."

Faith watched as her daughter wiped a tear, but then a smile tipped her lips. "Mommy, is it going to snow soon?"

"I think it's in the forecast."

Bella speared her salad with her fork. "Can

we make a snowman in the backyard like Daddy used to do?"

"Of course we can."

Her daughter's left eyebrow rose. "But can we make two instead of one—side by side?"

"I think it would be a great idea. We'll check out the weather on the computer later."

Bella tossed a few more miniature saltines into her chili before taking another bite. "What else did Daddy love?"

"Well, you know the rocking chair up in your bedroom?"

"The one Grandpa made when I was still in your tummy?"

She smiled. "Yes, that's the one. Your daddy loved to hold you in his arms and rock in that chair. He would sing softly until you fell asleep and then he'd watch you for hours."

Bella gazed toward the window. "Even though I never knew him, I miss Daddy."

Faith's heart ached for her daughter. "I know you do. I miss him, too. I'm sorry I've never talked about him with you before tonight."

Bella jumped out of her chair and climbed into her mother's lap. "It's okay—I know it makes you sad."

She kissed Bella's forehead. "Not anymore. What do you say if starting today, we talk about your daddy at least once a day? Even if it's to say how much we love him."

"Yes!"

Faith's heart soared at her daughter's excitement. "After we finish dinner, I thought you and I could go up into the attic and go through some pictures."

"You mean I can hold a picture of Daddy against my heart so he'll know how much I love him?" Bella wiggled loose from Faith's arms. "Let's go now!"

She'd brought a few to the table, knowing Bella would be too excited to wait. "We'll finish our dinner first, but you can look at a couple before we eat. I thought you could pick some of your favorites. Then we'd go shopping for some special frames for your bedroom. How does that sound?"

With a curious eye, Bella studied the photograph of her father in uniform. It was taken on the day of his graduation from the fire training academy. "Can I frame this one?"

Faith remembered every detail of the day. She'd woken up at three in the morning to an empty bed. She'd gone downstairs and found her husband at the kitchen table reading his Bible. She'd assumed he was too excited about starting work with the Whispering Slopes Fire Department. Instead, she'd found he was scared. As long as Faith had known him, he'd never expressed fear. Chris was a believer who trusted in the Lord. When she questioned him, he'd told her he was afraid to start a family because something terrible could happen to him.

"Can I, Mommy?"

Her child was beaming. Guilt swept in like a rushing tide. She'd been so wrong. Bella missed her father just as much as she missed her husband. She'd deprived her daughter of the chance to know him. "Yes, you can have as many pictures as you'd like."

Chapter Seven

Saturday, with the temperatures in the upper twenties and a brilliant, crystal clear sky, was a perfect day for the annual Whispering Slopes snowman-making contest.

"I can't believe you're going to be on a team with Joshua," Joy said as she helped Faith set up the concession stand in the afternoon. "I guess you two have put your differences aside."

She hadn't put anything aside. Her plan hadn't changed just because Joshua was helping with the meals. Faith had no doubt of his motives. "Not really." She pulled a stack of foam cups from a box under the table. "You can thank your niece for this awkward pairing."

Joy laughed. "I think it's cute. Of course, Joshua doesn't really strike me as a snowman-making kind of guy."

Faith knew why he'd agreed. "He's doing

it for Bella. For some reason, the two have some kind of connection." She placed a stack of paper plates on the table, next to the home-made caramel brownies. "I don't really get it, but Bella's happy."

"I think it's pretty obvious."

Faith tucked a strand of hair underneath her pink ski hat. "What?"

"Remember last year, when I dated Rick?"

Yes, the infamous Rick. Joy had met him at a teacher's conference in Richmond. The two hit it off and started a long-distance relation-ship lasting for over a year…until he'd proposed and Joy found she wasn't quite ready to give up her independence. "Of course I remember him, but what does he have to do with any of this?"

"Bella latched on to him. She wanted to be with him whenever he was in town."

Where was Joy going with this? "I'm sorry… I don't understand what Rick has to do with Bella's attachment to Joshua?"

"She wants a father figure in her life."

Faith knew that was what Bella prayed for every night, but it still smarted. "Don't you think Bella gets enough love at home?" The thought wrenched her heart.

Joy turned away from the snacks and toward her sister. "Oh, no, sweetie, that's not what I'm saying." She rubbed Faith's arm and smiled. "Bella gets more than enough love."

"Then why would you say something like that?"

The smell of burning firewood drifted past the table. Mr. Watson was getting ready to start roasting hot dogs and grilling hamburgers.

"It's a different dynamic, the relationship between a father and daughter. It has nothing to do with Bella not getting enough love from you."

Faith considered her sister's words, but didn't want to believe them. She looked up when she heard the familiar whistle. Through the snow glare bouncing off the table, she saw Bella skipping alongside Joshua, with her hand firmly planted in his.

"Yep...just like Rick," Joy said as she spotted the two.

"Mommy—look who's here."

Faith's breath hitched. Wearing aviator sunglasses, Joshua was dressed in black jeans and a camel leather jacket. He looked more like he was attending a modeling shoot than a day of building snowmen.

"Good afternoon, ladies."

"Hello," the sisters replied in unison.

"Bella, I thought you were going to help Mrs. Watson get some of the food ready?"

Faith eyed her daughter, who remained glued to Joshua's side.

"I gotta make sure Mr. Joshua is signed up on our team," Bella said before bolting off toward the registration table.

Silence lingered between the threesome.

"So, Joshua, with all of this cooking I hear you're doing, I take it you got the all-clear from the doctor?" Joy asked.

Faith exchanged a quick glance with him before he answered.

"Yes, I did. Your poor sister isn't saddled with taking care of me any longer, but now I've practically taken over her kitchen."

Faith grabbed a knife and ran it down the center of the chocolate sheet cake. "Caring for you wasn't a big deal. Actually, Mrs. Watson did more than me."

Joy eyed her sister. "Maybe not, but you have to admit it was stressful being back in the caretaking mode."

"Joy! Please…let's not talk about it."

Joshua looked back and forth at the two women. "I don't understand."

Joy cleared her throat. "I think he should know, sis."

"Know what?"

Faith shrugged her shoulders when Joy looked her way. She should never have told Joy about the meltdown at the hospital the other day. But her sister was intent on sharing how difficult the past several days had been. But why? What did she think would happen? Out of guilt or some sense of obligation, Joshua would hand over the inn? No chance of that happening.

"When Chris, her husband, was killed in the fire, Faith had just finished medical school and was starting her residency."

Faith's stomach turned over as she heard her sister's words. She wanted this to conversation to end. She'd give him the abbreviated version and be done with it. "I had to drop out because every time I stepped foot in the hospital, I had a panic attack." She sucked in her breath and released it. "There, now he knows. Are you happy, Joy?"

Joy rested her hand on her sister's arm. "I'm sorry, but he needs to know what you sacrificed by spending time in the hospital again. And the stress you were under by playing 'doctor' while he was under mandatory bed rest."

Joshua removed his sunglasses and turned his attention to Faith. His eyebrows crinkled together. "I had no idea."

Warmth radiated in his eyes, sending a shiver down her spine. "How would you?" She shrugged her shoulders. "My medical school days were a lifetime ago, so please, let's drop it."

Funny, no matter how many years had passed, the pain and humiliation remained. When she experienced her first panic attack in front of her classmates, she'd been mortified. The burn victim had just been brought into the ER and within seconds, she couldn't breathe. She fainted right there, in front of everyone. After the episodes continued, she knew she had no choice but to drop out of school. Aside from burying her husband, making the decision to give up her dream of medical school had been the hardest thing she'd ever done.

The thoughts faded when Bella returned to the table. Dressed in her white snowsuit, she looked like an adorable little bunny rabbit.

"Mommy, we need to check in." She grabbed Faith's hand and gave it a tug. "The contest is going to start soon."

Joy glanced at her watch. "Yes, you better get going. I'll man the table while you're gone." She bent down and gave her niece a kiss. "You have fun, okay?"

"I will. I hope we win!" Bella shouted as she ran across the field. Her pink boots slipped on the packed snow.

"Shall we go?" Joshua motioned for Faith to join him.

Deep inside her stomach, the butterflies were now like bats. First, she'd had to take care of him, and then she was forced to share her kitchen for the next month. Now she had to build a snowman with this man.

The snow crunched underneath their boots as they walked in silence, until Joshua stopped in his tracks. "Faith." He cleared his throat. "I want to apologize for putting you in an uncomfortable position."

She forced a laugh. "I think we can put our differences aside for an hour or two and help my daughter build a snowman."

"I'm not talking about the contest."

"What then?"

He kicked his boot into a chunk of ice. "I'm sorry you had to take care of me. If I'd known anything about your past, I would have stayed in the hospital to spare you any pain."

Faith's heart softened. Even though this man had a plan that would rip her world apart, his display of compassion was an unexpected surprise. "I appreciate it, but really, Joy shouldn't have said anything. It's no big deal."

But it was. She wasn't being honest with him or herself. It was a huge deal. She'd gone out of her way since Chris's death to avoid stepping foot inside that hospital. She pushed down the guilt bubbling inside. Last year, when Mr.

Watson had gotten sick with pneumonia, she'd never visited him. Thankfully, he'd understood why. After all, the Watsons were like her surrogate parents.

His smile was warm. "Well, it was to me."

She couldn't hold her tongue. "So if it was such a big deal, how is it you can take the only home Bella has ever known away from her—and me?" She placed her hand to cover her mouth. This wasn't the place. Why had she let her emotions take over?

Joshua's smile melted. "I have my own reasons for bidding on the inn, and trust me, they are nothing personal against you or Bella."

"Well, you can think whatever you'd like, but it's personal to me." She turned on her heel and headed toward her daughter and the other teams.

By the time Joshua placed the snowman's head on top of the middle ball, Faith had cooled down a bit. Today was about Bella. She was on top of the world and that was what mattered most.

"Can I put the coal eyes on, Mr. Joshua?" Bella asked, holding two lumps of coal and wearing a small lopsided smile.

Seeing her daughter so trusting of Joshua ignited a brief sense of security, which she'd lost the night of the fire. But why? He couldn't provide her with security—he was stealing it.

Joshua hoisted Bella up in the air and leaned her toward the snowman. "Go ahead...stick them on. He's anxious to see what his competition looks like." He turned and threw Faith a reassuring look.

Had he read her mind? Was he trying to calm her fears and comfort her? For a second, she wanted to think so. But those thoughts vanished when she thought of the inn and everything this man could steal from her. Her gut told her to guard her heart.

Monday morning, after the threesome had taken first prize in the snowman-making contest, Joshua found himself camped out at Faith's kitchen table. With the renovations under way and his to-do list a mile long, his priority today was to speak with Melissa about the trust fund. He'd left her a couple of messages after Joe had broken the news about his father cutting him off, but he hadn't heard from her. If he didn't have access to the funds, he'd have to apply for a loan, but he knew being currently unemployed could pose a problem. He hoped that with his detailed business plan for the new resort forecasting an earned profit almost immediately, his lack of employment wouldn't be an issue.

"So, what kind of experience do you have running an inn?"

Faith's question broke the silence and carried an accusing tone. Her brow arched as she stood next to the table with a fresh cup of coffee in her hands. So much for thinking that winning the contest would soften her a bit.

He moved his laptop aside and folded his hands together before resting them on top of the table. "I have years of business experience, which qualifies me to run a place like the Black Bear. In fact, I have enough confidence in my ability that I plan to expand the inn."

She slipped into the chair opposite him. "What do you mean? It's fine just the way it is."

He'd had a feeling she'd express some opposition to any sort of remodeling, having spent her childhood under the roof of the inn. He sucked in a breath. There was no point in keeping it a secret. She'd find out anyway, once he got the property and the building started. "I plan to build condos, maybe a little restaurant and some shops."

Her face turned to stone. "You can't build condos. And the restaurant…it's being remodeled now. Why would you want to build something new?"

"I don't think you understand my plans. I want to redevelop the land to make the Black Bear Inn a high-end resort. In fact, my idea could make it the best on the—" He cringed at his own words, which sounded like his father speaking. As a teenager, he'd vowed to be nothing like his father. "I believe it could be quite successful. Not to mention it could lead to an economic boom in the area."

Faith's finger circled the top of her mug. "You obviously know nothing about this community. We don't need or want something on such a grand scale."

Joshua leaned his back against the chair and crossed his arms. "It's apparent you don't know the first thing about what's best for your community. Think of all of the revenue a place like what I have in mind could generate—roads could be improved, new schools built. Perhaps you should put your personal feelings aside and think like someone with business sense."

He'd gone too far. Her silence was proof, but he wanted to make a point. And judging by her glare, he'd done just that.

"I'm glad we had this conversation." Her statement was abrupt but her voice quivered. "If you'll excuse me, I have to go to the store. I'll be back in time to help you with lunch."

"I do the shopping—remember? It was part

of the original plan." He pushed himself away from the table.

"No. Joy and I are planning Bella's party. Her birthday is two weeks from Saturday." She strolled to the sink and rinsed her cup. Releasing a heavy breath, she turned around and their eyes connected. "I wouldn't get your heart set on your grand plan."

"And why is that?"

"I won't allow anyone to change the inn—ever." She grabbed her purse and was out the door in a flash.

The icemaker churned as Joshua tried to shake off the frosty chill in the air Faith had left behind. The tension between them was growing and he couldn't help wondering how much longer he'd be able to use her kitchen to prepare the meals for the inn. Perhaps he should investigate other possibilities. Maybe he could use the kitchen at the church. He made a mental note to call once he spoke with Melissa. He picked up his phone, scrolled to her name and hit Call.

"Hello, this is Melissa Ferguson."

Sounds of papers shuffling echoed through the phone. "What's with the formalities?"

"Oh—hey, Joshua."

"You sound a little stressed. Are you okay?"

"Joann's been on vacation this week. I didn't

realize how much she does. Remind me to give her a raise when she returns."

Joshua strummed his fingers on the oak table. "You've got a great assistant. I'm glad you realize it. Did you get my message?"

She blew a heavy breath into the phone. "Yes, I'm sorry. I planned to call you as soon as your father's attorney sent over the paperwork, but it's been crazy."

"No problem—I've been a little busy myself."

"Yeah, I heard the auction has been delayed due to a fire." The clicking of a keyboard sounded. "That's too bad."

Melissa was obviously completely distracted. For a second, he considered calling back once Joann returned, but he needed to know what was going on. "So, I assume Joe told you?"

"Yes, he called about your trust and mentioned the fire."

He hesitated as he swallowed hard. "So what's the deal? Joe said my father cut me off. Is it true?"

"Yes, I'm afraid so. He had a clause that the trust would become null and void if you ever left his company."

His shoulders slumped. After speaking with Joe the other day, Joshua had hoped somehow this was all a big mistake—but it wasn't. He should have known something like this would happen.

And it was all about the inn.

After all, the reason Joshua had walked out of his father's office was a fight about the Black Bear Inn. And his mother, who'd had dreams of expanding the inn. She'd wanted to turn her favorite spot on earth to an even grander place for families to visit from all over the world.

His father? He'd had other ideas.

His mother had come to him in tears when she'd overheard her husband had plans to sell her beloved inn. He'd been eyeing another property in the Shenandoah Valley that he believed could make more money. Joshua had stormed into his father's office and accused him of being a terrible husband and of putting his business before his own wife. He'd told his father he'd never work for him again. "You'll regret this." His father's last words rang in his ears and continued to play over and over long after he'd bolted from the room. Even more so after his mother's death.

"Are you still there, Joshua?"

His jaw tightened. Two days later, his wife had left. The only thing she left behind was a note accusing him of leading them down a path to the poorhouse by quitting his job. She'd never cared about him—only his money.

"Josh?"

"Yes, I'm still here and this is exactly where I plan to stay." He ended the call more determined than ever to fulfill his mother's dream—even without his trust.

But how?

Chapter Eight

"It's nine thirty. Where is Mr. Bryson?" Faith asked her sister as she paced the pine floor of the First National Bank of Allegheny early on Thursday morning. With her patience wearing thin and the tension between her and Joshua the last couple days, she felt emotionally drained. When he'd suggested doing the cooking at the church, the idea sounded blissful, but in the end, she needed to help with the meals and shuffling back and forth to the church with Bella wasn't an ideal situation.

She walked toward the serving cart, picked up the pitcher of water and poured herself a drink. After gulping down half of it, she set the glass down with force. "I've got a lot to do today. I can't be wasting time waiting on him."

Joy sat patiently with a cup of coffee, eyeing her twin. "Well, I see you're all back to normal…impatient as ever. You need to slow down and relax. Didn't what happened yesterday teach you anything?"

Yesterday evening, Joy had rushed her sister to the doctor after she'd complained of dizziness. He'd said it was probably stress-related. But later, a test of her blood sugar had indicated elevated levels that required monitoring.

Faith stopped in her tracks. "You heard the doctor—there's nothing wrong with me."

"That's not exactly what he said. Besides, you didn't see your face. You were white as snow. I think you should have a second opinion…maybe see another specialist over in Davis."

A nerve twittered in Faith's jaw. She didn't have time to go from town to town to umpteen doctors who'd probe and prod her. She needed a loan and she needed it fast. The auction would be here before she knew it, and she had to be prepared. "I don't need a specialist. Don't you remember Grandmother dealing with blood sugar issues? It's hereditary."

Tugging her ponytail holder off, she cascaded her hair over her shoulders. When the main entrance door chimed, Faith whirled around. Her eyes widened at the sight of Joshua strolling into the bank…her bank. Why was he here? This man seemed to show up everywhere.

Seconds trickled as he appeared to move in slow motion toward her. He wore gray dress slacks and his chocolate brown leather coat. His clean-shaven face highlighted a strong jaw. The scent of peppermint caused her heart to batter her rib cage.

Faith stood frozen when he stopped in front of her and extended his hand.

"Well, hello there."

His voice sounded as smooth as her favorite ice cream. A warm sensation ran up her arm when their hands touched. What was that? She shook off the feeling.

"I hope you're doing better today."

She tried to speak, but the words seemed lodged in her throat. Faith was grateful when her sister stepped forward.

Joy approached Joshua. "She's doing a lot better. Thank you again for covering dinner by yourself last night, and breakfast this morning."

Both Joy and Joshua turned toward Faith. Her cheeks burned as they continued to stare. Say something…anything. She willed her fat tongue to get out of its own way so she could speak. "Ah…ah…yes, thank you." There, she said it. Now she just wanted to run from the building and take refuge in her safe little cottage. She didn't like the effect Joshua was having on her. Whatever it was it had to stop.

Once again, Joy took control of the conversation. "So what brings you to the bank?"

He flashed a sparkling smile, causing Faith to take a step back. "I have a nine-thirty appointment with Mr. Bryson, the vice president."

No way. This couldn't be happening. A wave of dizziness tried to take hold, but Faith fought it off. "It couldn't be. I'm meeting with him then."

Joshua removed his phone from his jacket, tapping it a few times. "No, see, it's right here on my calendar."

Faith's eyes quickly scanned the device when he flashed it in her face. There it was…just as he'd said. "You're a guest in this town, why would you need to meet with the vice president of our bank?" Her gut cinched—she knew why.

"Mr. Carlson?"

There was no time for Joshua to answer. Faith turned as Mr. Bryson's assistant approached, dressed in a pin-striped pantsuit and her hair in a tight bun.

"Yes, that's me."

"I have to apologize. There's been a little confusion with the scheduling," the woman stuttered.

"Yes, Ms. Brennan and I were just discussing the mix-up." He glanced in Faith's direction and then back to the assistant. "I'm in no rush, so please, let her go first."

Faith couldn't help questioning his motives. Still, she needed to speak with Mr. Bryson, and the sooner the better. She had to know where she stood. "Thank you, Joshua. Are you ready, Joy?"

Her twin's eyebrows scrunched. "You want me in the meeting?"

Faith nodded. "Of course I do. After all, you took the day off from work to be here."

"Okay, then, ladies, let's get you back to Mr. Bryson's office." The woman's heels clicked along the floor as Faith and Joy followed behind.

Once inside the office, Faith wiped the beads of perspiration dotting her forehead. She dug her heels into the Oriental rug positioned in the center of the room, ready to state her case.

Fifteen minutes later, Faith couldn't believe what she was hearing. "So you're denying my application for the loan? But why?"

Her sister reached across the round cherry conference room table and squeezed her hand before Faith turned her attention back to Mr. Bryson. She wouldn't cry, not here, but how could she not? The dream she shared with Chris was slowly dying and there didn't seem to be anything she could do about it.

Mr. Bryson cleared his throat as he rose and walked to the sidebar. He picked up the pitcher of ice water and poured a full glass. "Would either of you like some?" he asked as he turned to face the sisters.

"No, thank you," they replied in unison.

He strolled back to the table and took a seat. "I'm so sorry, Faith, but it's just too big of a risk."

"But the Black Bear Inn has always been successful." She had to make him understand. She needed the inn. It was the only way to secure her daughter's future and her own.

He fingered through the stack of papers in front of him. "That's true, but it's been owned by another party all of those years."

Joy spoke up. "But Faith runs the place. She's handled a lot of their financial and social obligations."

Her sister's words in her defense warmed Faith's heart… Joy was always her number one supporter.

Mr. Bryson eyed the two women over his Coke-bottle glasses. "Being in charge and having a financial investment in a company are two different things. Since you rent a home on the property, you don't have any collateral. But more important, you didn't include any type of business plan with your application."

But she and Chris did have a plan. Of course it consisted of ideas scribbled into spiral notebooks, but together, it was a plan. When her lip began to quiver, she knew it was time to go. She pushed herself away from the table. "Thank you, Mr. Bryson. I'm sorry I wasted your time this morning." She quickly turned and raced from the room.

"Faith, wait!"

The plea from her sister went ignored. The walls of the financial institution were closing in. She had to get out of here before she completely fell to pieces. Turning the corner at full speed, she slammed straight into her nemesis.

"Faith...what's wrong?" Joshua gripped her arms to steady her.

She pulled herself loose, but the tears gushed before she could make her escape. "This is your fault," she yelled as she ran toward the front entrance.

"Faith! Wait—talk to me."

Outside, the frigid air smacked her in the face as she rushed to the car. He was the last person she wanted to talk to, and now he'd witnessed her meltdown.

Faith popped the lock on the SUV and slipped behind the wheel. Before she could lock the door, Joshua was beside her in the passenger seat, smelling like peppermint.

"Please, Faith, tell me what's wrong. Maybe I can help."

She couldn't look at him, but she felt his eyes searing the side of her face as he waited for her to answer. Glancing out the window, she spotted Joy leaving the bank. Since they'd driven together, she willed her sister to walk faster. When she abruptly stopped in her tracks and turned around, Faith knew she'd seen Joshua. Her breath hitched when Joy disappeared through the front entrance.

With the palms of her hands, she wiped the tears streaming down her face. Her mascara was probably staining her cheeks, but she didn't care. When she turned, their eyes locked and his sympathy was evident. For a moment, she believed he cared, but the thought melted like the snow on her windshield, which was fast disappearing from the heat of the defroster.

"You can't help me...no one can." She reached inside her purse for a tissue, but the package was empty. "Please, will you just go?"

When his hand covered hers, she relaxed and the tears slowed. His touch was soothing. She felt safe. How could she feel this way in the presence of the man who was destroying her dream?

"Talk to me, Faith."

She jerked her hand away from his tender

touch. He was the enemy. It didn't matter to him that her dream was disintegrating right before her eyes. Without the loan, she couldn't move forward. This would be good news to the man sitting next to her, pretending he cared. She sucked in a deep breath and glared into his eyes. "I need for you to get out of my car."

Ten minutes later, Joshua found himself once again in the lobby of the bank, waiting for his appointment with the vice president. The second he'd stepped out of her car, she'd peeled out toward the entrance where Joy stood waiting for her. He couldn't get the look on Faith's face out of his mind. There was no question about it—the woman despised him. How could he fault her for that? But underneath the anger coating her eyes was disappointment. He could only guess she'd come to the bank for a loan and she'd been declined.

He, on the other hand, would not be denied. With his business plan organized inside the leather portfolio resting on his lap, he breathed a sigh of relief, realizing Faith was most likely out of the way. He'd just taken another step in the direction of owning the inn, as long as a multitude of other investors didn't come out of the woodwork. Guilt gnawed at his insides. He'd have to keep his mother at the forefront of his mind and forget about Faith. He had to admit, if only to himself, that getting her out of his mind was becoming increasingly difficult.

Twenty minutes into his meeting with Mr. Bryson, Joshua felt more confident than he had since he'd walked away from his job with his father. Run away was more like it.

"You've got a great business plan here, Joshua. There's no question about it—you have your father's head when it comes to business."

He cringed at the man's words. Joshua didn't want to resemble his father in any way, shape or form. His father was nothing but a ruthless businessman who'd always put his own needs before his family. He couldn't count how many times his father had told him he'd never do well in the business world if he didn't toughen up. But to Joshua, if being tough meant hurting the ones you loved, success wasn't important.

"So does that mean I've got the loan?"

Mr. Bryson closed the portfolio and slid it back in front of Joshua, extending his hand. "You got it. I'll draw up the paper and have them couriered over to the inn."

The last thing he wanted was for Faith to intercept the documents. "Why don't you just give me a call once they're ready? I'd be happy to come here to sign and have everything notarized."

Mr. Bryson nodded. "Fine, whatever you'd prefer. I must say I was surprised to hear your father wanted to sell the inn. I know how much your mother loved the place."

He was relieved Mr. Bryson didn't ask why his father didn't gift him the inn. "That's exactly the reason I want to keep it in the family, sir."

"Very well." The man rose from the table and gave a departing handshake. "It's a pleasure to work with you, Joshua. I wish you all the best with the auction."

"Much appreciated. I'm praying for a low turnout to keep the bidding down." He released his grip.

"It's a popular spot. Don't be surprised if you find yourself caught up in a bidding war, Joshua." He fingered his tie as he led his customer out into the lobby.

Inside his car, Joshua considered Mr. Bryson's mention of a bidding war. It was the last thing he needed. He slid the key into the ignition and headed to the grocery store. For lunch, he planned to cook pasta and garlic bread along with a side salad. After her episode at the bank, the thought of being alone in the kitchen with Faith didn't sit well with him. Would she ask him about his appointment? He hoped not. His guilty conscience had already taken a good beating.

At the market, he grabbed a shopping cart after noting the time. He needed to make this a quick stop if he wanted to get lunch served at its regular time.

He rounded the aisle, heading toward the pasta.

"Joshua!"

Turning, he spotted Joy speeding her cart toward him.

"Hi, Joy. I'm in a bit of hurry. My appointment at the bank went a little longer than I anticipated."

She glanced at her watch. "Oh, yes, we're nearing the lunch hour. I won't keep you." Reaching inside her purse, she slipped out an envelope and handed it to him.

He accepted it and noticed his name on the front, obviously written by a child using a red crayon. *Mr. Joshua.* He smiled, knowing who it was from.

"It's an invitation to Bella's birthday party. She wanted me to make sure I hand-delivered it to you."

He peeled it open and pulled out the card. He grinned as he studied a picture of Snoopy across the front.

"The party is two weeks from this Saturday.

We've rented out the community center. She'd really like it if you'd come."

Without hesitating, he answered. "I wouldn't miss it for the world." He smiled as he slid the invitation back inside of the envelope. "Does Faith know she invited me?"

Joy rested her hand on his arm. "Don't worry about my sister. It's Bella's party and I told her she could invite anyone she wanted. You were first on her list."

"She's a special little girl." Whether Faith wanted him at the party or not, he'd show up for the child. She'd already experienced too many disappointments in her young life.

"She sure is." Joy paused for a moment and tugged on her ear. "Listen, I wanted to apologize for anything Faith may have said to you earlier at the bank. She's been under a lot of stress lately with the inn going up for auction. Being turned down on her loan today was a hard blow for her."

He nodded. "There's no need for an apology." He knew Faith wanted the inn as badly as he did. The news today had to have been upsetting for her.

Joy stepped in a little closer. "I know you really want the inn for business reasons, but for Faith, it's so much more. I only hope she'll share the reason with you before it's too late."

At the checkout lane, Joshua replayed his conversation with Joy. He could have argued his plans to own the inn were not driven by business, but what would be the point? Still, what she'd said gnawed at him. What was Faith's reason? More than likely, he'd never know since he couldn't imagine she'd ever share it with him. As much as he hated to admit it, time was running out for Faith and her dream of owning the inn.

Chapter Nine

Faith paced the floor of her kitchen like a caged animal. Her stomach turned over as she glanced at the clock on the stove. Joshua would be here soon to prepare lunch. She'd thought about heading up to the inn to avoid him. No— to hide. But she'd have to face him sooner or later. She'd felt like such a fool, earlier at the bank. Of all people, he had to be there to witness her reaction to being denied by the bank.

A cold draft drifted across the room as a northerly wind howled against the window. Perhaps a cup of chamomile tea would calm her nerves. While the flame danced underneath the kettle, she gazed at Chris's picture hanging on the wall. Bella wanted it hung there so she'd feel like her daddy was sitting at the table with them.

Faith pulled her eyes away from the photo

when the kettle whistled. At the stove, she filled her mug and bobbed the tea bag up and down in the boiling water. When she looked over at the kitchen table, the reality of her situation took hold. The loan papers strewn in front of her, stole her breath.

Shoulders slouched, she walked to the table and slid into the chair. *What should I do, Chris? I didn't get the loan.* With tears peppering her eyes she looked toward the photograph for an answer. Minutes later, she knew. Chris had prepared for the worst when he took out the large insurance policy on his life. He wanted to make sure his family was well cared for. Now it was up to Faith to take control and give her daughter the security she deserved. She knew exactly what had to be done.

Her heart thumped against her chest as she picked up the phone and called Joy.

"Do you still want to help me?" Faith blurted, not giving her sister a chance to say hello.

A moment of silence passed. "Are you talking about Bella's birthday party? Look, I'm sorry if you're angry I let Bella invite Joshua."

Faith crinkled her brow. "What? No—I'm not talking about her party. Do you want to help me buy the inn? You know, be partners."

"But, sweetie, you didn't get the loan."

She certainly didn't need to be reminded of

that fiasco. "I know I didn't. I've decided I'm going to use some of the insurance money. I kept telling myself it's for Bella's future, but the inn is her future—it's both of ours. If I use the money, I'll be giving Chris his dream, too."

"I couldn't agree with you more, sis."

The heavy weight pressing on her chest for days had finally eased. Faith knew she was making the right decision. "I'd like to keep some of the insurance money as our nest egg, so that's where you come into play."

"You don't have to ask. My offer to loan you the money still stands. I like the idea of us being partners. Of course I'd be the silent one."

Outside, a car door slammed. For a moment, she'd almost forgotten about Joshua. Her heartbeat skipped. "Let's discuss the details later. Joshua just pulled up."

"Be nice. Remember, he's doing you a favor cooking all of these meals."

Faith ended the call. He might be helping her out, but he was benefiting, too. In his mind, the inn was already his and he had to take care of the current customers if he wanted them to return or to give referrals.

Setting her teacup on the counter, she strolled toward the gentle knock at the door. A strange sense of calmness covered her like a warm blanket as she let him in. She couldn't wait to tell him he still had competition in his quest for the inn.

"Sorry I'm late—my meeting ran a little long." Joshua stepped inside and carried the bags of groceries to the kitchen table. "I'm making pasta and salad, so I'll be quick and get out of your hair."

As soon as she saw his face wearing an arrogant smirk, she knew he'd gotten the loan. She reached into one of the bags to help unload the supplies. She eyed him as he pulled out the oversize pot and carried it to the sink. He turned on the spigot as she continued to watch him. Not knowing if he was going to bring up her meltdown at the bank, she decided she'd beat him to it.

"I'm sorry about my behavior at the bank." She hesitated for a moment as she placed two heads of lettuce onto the table. "I didn't mean to drag you into the middle of it."

Joshua turned off the water and turned to face her. "There's no need to apologize. It's upsetting to be denied a loan."

Her body froze. Did Mr. Bryson tell him he'd denied her or was her behavior alone enough to give him a heads-up?

The smirk faded. "I ran into Joy at the market. She mentioned it's why you were so upset. I kind of figured, though." He looked at her and a tiny smile tugged at the corner of his mouth. "I have to say, you look like a different person now. You're practically glowing."

She continued unloading the bag. "I am?" With the last of the groceries unpacked, she walked to the countertop. Now who was wearing the smirk? "Well, I guess I have reason to be. In a couple of weeks, I'll be the proud owner of the Black Bear Inn."

His cell phone chirped, but he ignored it. "I'm sorry. I don't understand. Joy said Mr. Bryson denied your loan."

"Yes, it's true. But I had a backup plan and it's going to make my dream come true." She grabbed her jacket and turned. "I'll be up at the inn. Call me if you need help bringing the food over." She closed the door behind her and smiled. Joshua Carlson actually looked a little nervous, but she was cool as a cucumber.

Later in the evening, with Bella tucked in bed, Faith curled up in her favorite comfy chair in the corner of her bedroom. The lights from the inn were shining through the opened plantation shutters. Could she really bring Chris's dream and hers to fruition? She smiled at the idea.

"Mommy, I can't sleep."

Faith turned at the sound of her daughter's sweet voice. Her heart warmed at the sight of

Bella in her pink-and-white polka-dot footie pajamas. "Come here and nuzzle with me."

Bella climbed into her mother's lap.

Faith stroked the tousled ringlets. The smell of baby powder penetrated her nose. The scent had provided much comfort over the years. "What's the matter, honey?"

"I wish I had a daddy."

"Oh, sweetie, I know you do." Had the photographs prompted this? Perhaps she should have kept them locked away. "Did you have a dream?"

She yawned and shook her head. "No, I was looking at the picture where Daddy was holding me at the hospital."

"That's nice, isn't it?" Faith remembered it as though it were yesterday. Chris had been thrilled to have a little girl. He'd told her he had hoped for a girl throughout her pregnancy. He wanted to have a "mini" Faith. "He was so proud of you."

The tears escaped and raced down Bella's soft, pink cheeks. "Why did he die? Why didn't God take care of him?"

"I don't know, sweetie. Sometimes things happen that we can't explain. It doesn't mean God didn't love Daddy or us. You just have to remember you'll see him one day."

"In Heaven?" she whispered as she rubbed her sleepy eyes.

"Yes."

"But I need Daddy next week."

"What do you mean?"

"The father-daughter dance at school," she said with a sniffle. "It's next Friday."

Joy had mentioned the dance. She'd hoped for Bella's sake it wouldn't be a big deal. Now, she wondered how she could have been so insensitive. She should have talked with Bella. "I'm sorry. Have your friends been talking about it?"

She nodded her head slowly. "Yes—Mary did."

Her heart ached for her daughter. In the future, she'd experience all of these major life events without her father. So many times, Faith woke up consumed with thoughts of Bella's first date, her first breakup, graduation from high school and, most important, her wedding. "Maybe I can take you to the dance, sweetie."

Bella giggled softly. "You're not a daddy."

"I know I'm not, but they might make an exception and let a mommy come. Is there anyone else in your class without a daddy?"

"No."

Feeling helpless, Faith bit down on her lip.

"Mary says the daddy walks the daughter to get married. Who's gonna walk me?"

"I will, sweetie." She snuggled her nose into Bella's neck.

"Mary said if you married Mr. Joshua, he could. Do you think he'd take me to the dance?"

Faith's stomach lurched at her question. "Sweetie, Mr. Joshua is a very busy man."

Her eyes brightened. "What if he doesn't have anything to do that night?" Hope oozed from her eyes as she pleaded. "Can I invite him, please?"

"You don't want me to take you?"

"No, it's for daddies. We'd look funny dancing together."

"We do it together here all the time. What's the difference?" she asked, knowing Bella wasn't going to give up on her quest to have Joshua accompany her to the dance.

"No one can see us here. Please, can I please ask him?"

"I'll have to think about it, sweetie. If not, we'll do something really special the night of the dance."

Bella kissed Faith on the cheek. "Good night, Mommy."

Faith knew her daughter wasn't happy with her answer. "Go say your prayers and I'll come tuck you in shortly."

Bella climbed off her lap. Without another word, she slowly walked back to her bedroom, her slippers scuffing across the hardwood.

Faith pressed her fingers to her temples. She didn't have a good feeling about this. He'd probably say yes to her invitation, afraid to hurt her feelings, but what kind of message would it send to Bella? As her mother, she couldn't let her daughter live in some fantasy world consisting of a future with Joshua as her father.

Joshua glanced at his watch—4:30 p.m. He'd finally reached the bottom of his to-do list. It had been a crazy Friday that started early this morning with several conferences calls with reputable contractors from the DC area. After Faith had informed him of her plan B, he was moving full steam ahead, hoping to be the highest bidder at the auction. Who knew, maybe once the dust settled, Faith would agree to come and work for him.

Maybe.

His emotions bubbled as he entered the Shenandoah Mall. Jessica lived to go to the mall—just another reason why she needed a man with a fat bank account. Not him. He'd quickly hit the biggest department store and scour the men's department for a couple new dress shirts, a few sweaters and some dress slacks. He had a roast in the oven for the guests, so he'd have to hurry.

As he strolled past the perfume counter, he turned in the direction of a familiar giggle. There was Bella squirting Faith with a tester bottle she'd grabbed from the counter. Stepping behind a nearby mannequin, he watched the mother and daughter as they moved down the counter and into the accessories area.

Faith grabbed a large floppy hat and plopped it on Bella's head. Bella, in turn, reached for a pair of oversize sunglasses. She slid them over her tiny face and began to imitate a model walking down the runway. When he laughed, a little too loud, they both turned in his direction.

Bella smiled wide as she raced toward him. "Mr. Joshua! What are you doing in the ladies' department?"

Faith approached him—her cheeks crimson.

"I was headed back to the men's clothing and I heard your distinctive giggles."

"What's stinctive?"

He rubbed the top of Bella's hat. "It means it could only belong to you."

Faith slid her hands inside the pocket of her black denim jeans. "We were just messing around...you know, girl stuff."

His pulse sped, which was becoming a common occurrence in her presence. He blamed it on the tension over the inn, but wondered if there was more to it. "Well, don't let me interrupt. I need to pick up a few dress shirts and pants." He felt a slight tug on the sleeve of his leather jacket and looked down at Bella.

She removed the sunglasses. Her eyes were like saucers. "If you're still here next Friday…"

"Bella!"

Joshua and Bella jumped at the sound of Faith's voice. The elderly woman at the perfume counter turned toward the commotion.

Faith shook her head. "No."

Bella's lip quivered as Joshua knelt down in front of the little girl. Her hand shook when he placed it in his. He gave Faith a quick glance and turned his attention back to the child. "What is it? It's okay, you can ask me."

Bella looked to her mother, who responded with a defeated shoulder shrug.

When one lone tear ran down Bella's face, his heart squeezed. He hated to see her in pain. "What about next Friday?"

She wiped her eyes with her other hand. "If you're still in town—" She paused, sniffed once and then again. "Would you take me to the father-daughter dance at my school?"

Joshua's thoughts drifted to his own childhood and the annual father-son softball game. His father had never showed. Not once. One year, he'd promised he'd be there to see his son pitch the opening inning, but as the hours passed and the sun began to set, there'd been no sign of him. Another empty promise had gone into the bottomless pit of disappointments. After all these years, the pain of watching all his friends with their fathers still caused a dull ache deep inside his stomach.

Without looking at Faith, he made his decision. "Of course, I'll go with you." There was no way he'd inflict pain on this child, like his father had done to him over and over. "I'm honored you asked me."

Her face lit up like thousands of fireflies in an open meadow on a steamy summer night. Her mother, on the other hand, didn't look too happy. Bella threw her arms around his neck. "Oh, thank you, Mr. Joshua." She pulled back and peered at him. "We'll have fun—I promise." Bella turned to her mother. "Mommy, can I go try on some more hats?"

Faith scanned the hat area a few feet away. "Yes, but don't wander off. I need to speak with Mr. Joshua, and then we need to get back to the inn."

"Okay, bye, Mr. Joshua." The girl turned and skipped toward the accessories, whistling.

"You didn't have to say yes," Faith said as she kept an eye on her daughter.

"There's no way I'd turn down her invitation."

Faith pushed away a strand of hair that fell on her face. "That's kind of you. I know how busy you are."

He knew the mall wasn't exactly the best place to talk about the auction, but since she'd mentioned her plan yesterday, he hadn't been able to get it off his mind. "Well, I guess you're busy, too, with this plan B you were so excited about yesterday. Care to share it with me?"

She threw her shoulders back. "Now, why would I do that—you're my enemy."

His eyes narrowed. Was it really what she thought of him? It was true they both wanted the inn, but it seemed a little harsh. "I'm sorry you feel that way."

"It's exactly how I feel. I'm prepared for a fight. I'm not going to give up, if that's what you're hoping for."

Joshua studied her face. Even wearing a scowl, she was one of the most beautiful women he'd ever seen. For a moment, he wondered, if they weren't at odds over the inn, could a relationship develop? Who was he kidding? She couldn't stand him. Besides, she'd only break his heart as Jessica had done. "By the look on your face, you look like you could fight now."

"I just want to be clear on where I stand."

He nodded. "Oh, yes, you've been very clear.

Look, I know this is hard for you. The inn is not just your workplace but your home. Perhaps you can still work there after I take ownership—only if you want to."

Faith flipped her hair over her shoulders before placing both hands on her hips. "Work for you?" A blast of air blew through her lips. "That's not going to happen—ever."

"I just thought I'd put the offer out there. It seems your options are fairly limited in this area. I'd like to make sure you and Bella are taken care of."

"Feeling a little guilty, are you?"

Boy, was she fired up. He'd thought about presenting the option of her purchasing one of the condos he'd planned to have as rentals, but by the looks of the smoke coming out of her ears, now wasn't the time. "Not guilty—I'm just trying to help you. Remember, this isn't personal, Faith."

"We've been down that road already. I've got to go. I'll finish up with dinner. You don't need to come over." She turned on her heel, then stopped and faced him once again. "The dance is at seven on Friday. Do you want to meet her at the school?"

No matter their differences, when it came to Bella, he was going to do things right. "No, I'll pick her up—if it's okay with you, of course."

"That'll be fine." She turned and marched to her daughter.

Joshua watched the two head toward the door. He thought his plan was a good one. She could continue to work at the inn and if she agreed, she could live there, too. Nothing would change. As he continued to watch mother and daughter, his stomach twisted. Who was he kidding? Everything was about to change.

Chapter Ten

"Oh, that man makes my blood boil." Faith smashed the potatoes with the silver masher, using all her might. The early morning sun filtered through her kitchen window. For some reason, Joshua had insisted on making a traditional Thanksgiving feast for tomorrow's Sunday dinner. He'd said he'd take care of everything if she prepared the mashed potatoes. It seemed like a lot of work for one meal, but he'd insisted there'd be leftovers to use for lunch the following day. The man seemed to have an answer to everything—or at least he thought he did. Oh, brother.

"What man, Mommy?"

Oops. She'd forgotten Bella was at the kitchen desk, coloring. "Why don't you go back and practice your organ, sweetie? Aunt Joy and I have some business to discuss."

Bella did as she was told and carried her coloring book and crayons to her room. The door slammed and an off-key version of "Mary Had a Little Lamb" echoed down the hall.

Joy glanced toward Bella's room as she strolled toward the coffeepot. "It sounds…different." She poured herself a cup. "Maybe you should think about switching to decaf. You're wound as tight as a grannie's new perm this morning."

"I can't help it—he's so smug. He's walking around town like a peacock, convinced he'll be the new owner of the inn." Faith put the bowl aside and paced the floor with her arms wrapped around her waist. His confidence seeped through his pores. Each day it grew more and more difficult to open her kitchen to him.

"Joshua? Aren't you being a little harsh—a peacock?"

"Of course—him! The man I'm forced to see every day, right here under my own roof." She bit down hard on her lip. "Do you know he had the nerve to ask me to come to work for him? He'll probably expect me to rent some high-dollar, high-rise condos he thinks he's going to scatter around Whispering Slopes. Could you see me—in a condo of all places?" she laughed. "No thanks, I like my living space to touch the ground." The more she thought about it, the more her blood boiled. "He's so sure he'll get the inn he's already trying to hire employees—including me!"

"Maybe you misunderstood?"

"No, I didn't. He's feeling guilty he might put me out onto the streets. Well, he should have thought about it from the start. And if he's feeling so bad about it, why doesn't he just forget about the inn and go back to wherever he came from?" Why did he have to come here? Yes, the inn would have still gone up for auction, but this man is someone she wasn't sure she could compete with.

Joy clasped her hands together and rested them on the table. "I still think you should tell him the real reason the inn is so important to you."

"No! It's personal. He's the last person I'd want to know about our dream. That's between me and Chris."

She walked toward the table and sat down across from Joy. "Please, promise me you won't say anything to him...or anyone."

Joy nodded.

Bella's organ continued to echo down the hall with the sounds of an unfamiliar tune.

"Is there something else bothering you? You seem, I don't know...extra twitchy."

Ever since Joshua had accepted Bella's invitation, she'd had an uneasy feeling. She wanted to talk with Joy about it, but she'd been afraid of her reaction. What if she thought it was a good thing? She sucked in a long breath and, against her better judgement, began. "Yesterday, while Bella and I were at the mall goofing around in the accessories area, we ran into Joshua."

Joy snorted.

"What's so funny?"

"He's so manly, it's hard to picture him strolling through the accessories department."

Faith swatted her sister's arm. "Oh, brother... can you just stay with me here?" She did have to admit Joshua was masculine and protective—especially when it came to Bella.

"Sorry—go on."

"Bella was so excited to see him." She remembered the look on her daughter's face. How her eyes lit up the moment she saw him, making Faith's heart squeeze. "It was sad."

"Why?"

"She's getting so attached. She's getting her hopes up that somehow, he'll be someone permanent in her life...unlike her own father. The last thing I want is for her to be disappointed when he leaves."

Joy tilted her head. "Have you ever thought about the possibility he won't?"

She couldn't think about that. If she did, it would mean she'd lost her home. He had to leave. "Well, he's certainly not going to remain in town after I purchase the inn at the auction."

"Sis, I don't want you to set yourself up for disappointment. Remember, this guy comes from money. He probably has a huge trust fund."

She refused to let her sister's words cloud her mind. "I'm not worried about it."

"Okay, sorry to be a Debbie Downer. I just thought I'd remind you. Go on, Bella was excited and then what happened?"

Faith leaned back and gripped the smooth edge of the table. "She invited him to go with her to the father-daughter dance next Friday." Her chest ached at the words, but more because of his answer. "And he agreed to go."

Silence hung in the air as Joy digested the information.

"You know what the funny thing is? He even seemed kind of excited about it."

Joy's eyes bulged. "Oh, my—this is huge."

"Why?"

She twisted a loose tendril of hair around her finger. "It means he's getting as attached to Bella as she is to him…and maybe to you, as well."

Faith shook her head. "I seriously doubt the

latter." He didn't strike her as a man who'd let anything get in the way of his business ventures. Perhaps it was why he was still single and didn't have a family.

"But don't you sense he's at least a little attracted to you?" Joy asked before taking a sip of her coffee. "I definitely see it."

"The only thing I am to him is an obstacle in his path to owning the inn."

Joy shook her head. "I don't believe that. What about the day you ran out of the bank? He followed you and got into your car. He was obviously concerned."

She'd tried to block the day out of her mind. Being denied a loan was one thing, but for Joshua, of all people, to have witnessed her meltdown...that was even worse. She'd been mortified. "Doubtful—look, he knows what he's doing is wrong. He only came after me to make himself look better. The man couldn't care less about me."

"Well, either way, I think it's sweet Bella invited him. Imagine the pain of hearing all your little girlfriends chattering about the dance, and you can't go because you don't have a daddy. It's heartbreaking."

Faith knew how much this meant to Bella, but she couldn't help thinking this sent the wrong message to her. "So what happens if they do go together and she has a great time?"

"What on earth would be wrong with that?"

"Then he leaves town, leaving me with a brokenhearted little girl." The thought turned her stomach upside down.

The cordless phone chirped. Faith pushed herself out of the chair and glided across the hardwood toward the desk. "Hello?"

"Faith, it's Joshua." His tone was smooth, yet unsettling.

"Hey, what's up?" Her voice cracked.

"I've been thinking about Bella's invitation."

Great, he'd finally come to his senses. This was a big fat mistake. She'd been a fool to ever consider it. "Yes?"

"I thought you might be a little uncomfortable, you know, with me picking Bella up and driving her to the dance. After all, it's not as though you know a lot about me, other than the fact that I can cook."

Yes—her thoughts exactly. He could be on *America's Most Wanted*. His picture might be posted on the wall of their post office. She'd have to phone Betty, the postmaster, to check for her. Of course, the idea of him being a wanted man seemed a little far-fetched. He appeared to be a good person despite his intentions to ruin her life.

Joshua continued. "I thought maybe I could pick up you and Bella."

Did he mean both of them? She pulled the phone away and rubbed her ear. "I'm sorry, I didn't catch that."

"I thought the three of us could go to dinner before the dance."

"Together?" Was this his way of asking her on a date? She wasn't ready to go out with men. She'd come to the conclusion recently that she may never be. How could she ever build a new life with someone? All her memories of Chris would fade into oblivion. She'd never want him to think he was so easily replaced—that their marriage had meant nothing.

He laughed. "Yes, we can grab a bite to eat, and then we can all go to the dance together." He hesitated. "Kind of like a family."

Together? Family? Was he serious? "Ah… I'm not so sure it's a good idea."

"Look, Faith, try and put your own feelings about me and the inn aside and think of Bella. We'll be doing it strictly for her and no other reason."

Why did this seem so important to him? Did he really care that much about a little girl's feelings…one he'd only known a couple of weeks? She had no answers, but her gut told her he was right. She knew how much Bella wanted to attend the dance. Swallowing hard, she accepted the fact that she had to do it for her daughter. "Okay."

"Great! I'll pick you both up at six."

Still stunned by her own answer, she placed the phone back on the charger. Joshua's excitement played over in her head. Then the words "a family" poured into her mind. Guilt covered her like the oppressive humidity of an August day in the South. Was she betraying Chris by accepting Joshua's invitation?

"I like your car, Mr. Joshua. The seat is really comfortable," Bella announced as the three headed to the restaurant. "And it smells like peppermint…just like you do," she added with a giggle.

He laughed at the sweet voice coming from behind him. He'd been looking forward to this night ever since Bella had invited him. He wasn't so sure about her mother, though.

His breath accelerated as he realized this was the first time a child had ever sat on his leather seats. As a young boy, the few times his father had let him ride in his car, he'd put towels down. *We've got to protect the leather.* He shook away the voice. *Not tonight.* "I'm glad you like it."

"How come you don't have any kids, Mr. Joshua?"

"Bella! That's not any of your business."

Faith leaned toward him. "I'm sorry, sometimes she blurts things out without thinking."

The question had caught him off guard, but he shook his head. "Don't worry about it, ladies. I don't have any children now, but it doesn't mean one day I won't be blessed with a houseful." He glanced in the rearview mirror and spotted Bella grinning.

Joshua hit the brake for a red light and watched the little girl as she gazed out the window.

"I wish you could be my daddy, Mr. Joshua."

"Bella!" Faith turned and grimaced at her daughter. "You need to learn not to say every thought passing through your head."

"But you always told me to tell the truth, and it's the truth." Bella crossed her arms, appearing satisfied with her response.

"I'm sorry if she embarrassed you."

Joshua couldn't restrain his smile. He wasn't the least bit embarrassed, but the redness filling Faith's cheeks told him she sure was. "Actually, her words made me feel good."

His self-confidence had taken a beating since

he'd quit his job and Jessica had left. Hearing Bella speak her heart, with her childlike innocence, was a nice change of pace.

Spotting the sign for The Wagon Wheel, he hit the turn signal.

"I love this place," Bella shouted from the back seat. "They have yummy desserts."

Joshua put the car into Park and unfastened his seat belt. "From what I read on the internet, their steaks aren't half bad, either."

He rounded to the passenger side and opened the door for Faith as Bella leapt from the vehicle. When he took Faith's hand to help her from the car, it was stiff. Bella's comments had obviously made her uncomfortable. Not him. He hadn't had such sweet words spoken to him since before his mother passed.

An hour and forty-five minutes later, with three overstuffed bellies, they entered the gymnasium at Bella's school. Joshua scanned the packed room. Balloons and rainbow-colored streamers hung from the ceiling. Music and chatter filled the air. A 1970s-style disco ball splashed flecks of flashing light on the walls. Across the floor, two long tables were lined with bowls of pink and yellow punch, along with an array of sugary treats.

"Boy, it's a big turnout." He turned to Faith. "I guess it's good I invited you so you could help chaperone." Truthfully, his reasons for the invitation were stirring up some conflicting emotions. Had it really been just for Bella? It had to have been. He certainly wasn't interested in a relationship. The pain he'd endured after his marriage broke up was enough to last him a lifetime. He shook away the thoughts. "Would anyone like some punch?" Joshua shouted over the music blasting through the nearby speakers.

"That would be nice," Faith answered, raking her fingers through the back of her hair. "It is a little warm in here."

Bella jumped up and down. "I'll have some, too."

Faith rolled her eyes at Joshua. "Just what she needs, more sugar."

"Ah…come on, it's a special night. I'll be right back with the punch."

Joshua weaved in and out of the crowd when his cell phone vibrated in his pocket. He reached for the device and scanned the screen. Melissa. His mood wasn't exactly conducive for a conversation with his lawyer, but she could have some new information on the auction. Unable to hear her inside the gym, he turned toward a nearby exit. The last thing he wanted was to have her hear music and begin interrogating him as to where he was and who he was with. Since Jessica had left him, he'd gotten vibes from Melissa that made him a little uncomfortable.

"Hey, Melissa, what's up?" A tractor trailer whizzed by, its engine roaring.

"That sounded like a freight train. Where are you?"

Here we go. "I had a little dinner at a steak house and just stepped outside." That was kind of true. "So what's going on?"

"Your father's attorney called. The auction has been officially scheduled for two weeks from tomorrow, so I thought I'd check in."

His pulse quickened. "That's great news. It's a little sooner than I'd anticipated."

"Your father is back in the country and he's ready to move forward. Is it a problem?"

Not for him, but he couldn't help thinking about Faith and Bella. In just a couple weeks, they'd be without a home. If only Faith weren't so stubborn, they could still live on the property, once the condos were built. When his mother's beautiful face flashed in his mind, those thoughts disappeared. "No, of course not." His voice cracked.

"I'm sure you're getting excited to take over the place." She paused for a moment, and then continued. "I've been thinking."

This can't be good. "About what?"

"What if I move up there and help you run

the place? I'm rarely in court. I could work from there."

Her words rammed him like a bumper car at a county fair. He'd learned years ago that it was best to be up-front with Melissa. If he wasn't direct, she'd twist things around in her own mind. He swallowed the lump in his throat in preparation. "I don't think it's a good idea."

"Why not?"

Think, man. "Well, I'm not exactly a shoo-in to get the inn."

"What's that mean?"

"Faith Brennan plans to bid, and she's going to be tough competition." He didn't know for sure if she'd actually bid. This was his best defense. Besides, Faith was determined, and she did say she had a plan B. If anyone could come up with the funds despite being denied the loan, she would.

"Faith? The woman who cared for you after the accident? The one you've been cooking for? Are the two of you dating or something?" Her voice shook.

"Yes—I mean, no, we're not dating, but she is the one who cared for me. She's got some strong family ties to the place, and she's determined to gain ownership."

He could almost hear her wheels turning, devising a plan of action. He knew her well.

"Well, I can lend you some money, so you'd be sure to outbid her. All the money my grandfather left me when he passed away is just sitting around collecting interest."

Joshua cringed. There was no way that would happen. "No—but thanks. I need to do this on my own." He had to show his father he was still a capable businessman and didn't need to rely on his trust or anyone else. Once the new resort was making money, maybe his father would finally be proud of him.

"What if I send someone up to bid against her?"

He scratched the side of his temple. "I'm not sure what you mean?"

"A bogus bidder, you know, to run up the price. Obviously, money is no object for you. Even though your father cut you off, you've still obtained the loan. Getting the funding probably won't be as easy for her."

Joshua squeezed his phone. "You can't be serious?"

"Of course I am. What's the problem?" she asked.

This coming from his attorney—unbelievable. "Aside from being completely dishonest, it sounds illegal, too."

"Don't worry. There are ways around it. Besides, I know how much the inn means to you."

Joshua had always known Melissa was tough when it came to business, but he didn't know she was capable of something so unscrupulous. She was untrustworthy—just like Jessica. If ever there was a time to cut her loose, it was now. She was trouble with a capital T. "Look, I don't think this is going to work any longer."

"What are you talking about?" She hesitated and a garbled voice sounded through the phone. "I've got to catch my train. I'll be up the day before the auction—we'll talk then about me moving to Whispering Slopes."

He sucked in a breath and released it. "Please—send me this month's bill. I'm going to find a new attorney."

"You're joking, right?"

Breaking ties with her would be more difficult than he'd imagined, but he knew it was the end of not only their business relationship but also a friendship, whether she accepted it or not. She'd crossed the line, and one thing he wouldn't tolerate was dishonesty. He'd had enough of that with Jessica later in their marriage, when she was unfaithful.

Without another word, the line went dead. It was just as well. What more could he say? Her idea to defraud Faith out of a chance to make her dreams come true had infuriated him. Yes, he wanted the inn, but he'd gain possession walking an honest path. His anger toward Melissa bubbled deep in his gut. But then, as he stood under a streetlight in the parking lot, he wondered if he was any different from Melissa?

Chapter Eleven

Early Saturday, Faith had to struggle to get Bella out of bed. After they'd come home from the father-daughter dance the previous night, Bella's feet had never touched the ground. Reading her a bedtime story had been next to impossible, with the five-year-old full of tales of her and Joshua twirling on the dance floor. Faith's heart had soared all evening as she'd watched her daughter. She'd never seen Bella so happy in her life.

As she wiped down the granite countertop, Faith peered out the window. The once-fat snowflakes were fine and coming down harder than when she'd dropped Bella off at the church earlier, to practice for the children's play. Since the snow predictions were for little or no accumulation, Bella would stay at the church for several hours before Joy picked her up for a sleepover. This was perfect timing, giving Faith an opportunity to tackle the mound of paperwork she'd brought over from the inn.

Thirty minutes later, her stomach twisted when she spied Joshua walking up the snow-laden path toward the house. When he'd dropped her and Bella off last night, he'd said he'd be over to cook lunch around ten. Glancing at the clock on the stove, she saw he was right on the dot. Feeling a little uneasy about being alone with him after Bella's remark wishing he were her daddy, she wondered if she should bring it up with him or not. She sucked in a deep breath when he softly knocked on the door.

Whish.

A strong, gusty wind ripped the doorknob from her grip and sent a blast of wet snow and ice into her face.

"Whew! It's getting pretty nasty out there. This should be great for business."

Of course, his mind was always on her inn. Why wouldn't it be? She stepped aside and motioned him inside. Even with the strong winds, she couldn't escape his sweet peppermint scent.

Plato zipped to the door, licking up the melted flakes dotting the hardwood.

Faith snapped her fingers and pointed toward the bed. "Plato, it's okay, go lie down."

She scurried over to the coffeepot while Joshua set three grocery bags on the table. "We've got a lot of cooking to do today," Faith said as she removed two large mugs from the cherry cabinet and poured them each a cup of brew.

"The coffee smells great—thanks," he said as he accepted her offering and took a slow sip.

"Do you want me to get the salad going while you prepare the casserole?" she offered, since she didn't know the first thing about making any of the fancy dishes he'd suggested last night for today's menu. Her specialty was baked mac and cheese. It had been one of Chris's favorites.

Unloading the bags, he looked over. "Sounds good to me. I picked up a couple of cucumbers and tomatoes, as well as some Italian dressing."

Thirty minutes later, the salad was made and the casserole bubbled inside the oven, filling the room with the aroma of garlic and oregano. They settled into the chairs at the kitchen table with a second cup of fresh coffee and some chocolate-nut biscotti. Icy pellets of snow flicked against the windows.

Faith cleared her throat as she traced her finger along the lip of her cup. "I wanted to say thank-you again for last night. You made Bella the happiest little girl in the entire Shenandoah

Valley. She was still chattering about it when I dropped her off at the church earlier."

"I should be thanking you for agreeing to the evening. Bella is such a special and compassionate child. Being around her brings so much joy into my heart." He paused and glanced toward the frosty window before turning his attention back to Faith. "She also reminds me of what my life is missing."

Moving forward after losing Chris in the fire had been the most difficult thing Faith had ever done. If it hadn't been for Bella, she wasn't sure she would have survived those early years. "Children are indeed a gift from God," she whispered.

"My wife—excuse me, ex-wife—left me for another man. We'd been married for five years. I wanted children, but she didn't." He ran his hand across his face. "I take it back. She didn't want children with me." A moment of silence passed through them. "I heard through a friend that she and her new husband recently had a little boy."

She touched her parted lips with her finger, not sure how to respond. Since they'd met, in her mind she'd seen him as a man who put business first, with no desire for a family. "I'm really sorry, Joshua. That must be hard for you."

"Honestly, when I first heard, I was happy for her."

"How could you be?"

"I always thought she'd make a wonderful mother. We had a good marriage for a couple of years…at least I thought we did. Other than the disagreements about having children, we never argued much. Before I quit my job, she seemed happy—I know I was. I'd accepted the fact I'd never be a father and I was okay with it because I loved her so much. When I made the decision to leave my job, she lost all respect for me—I guess I can't really blame her. She grew up with money and wanted a man who'd take care of her financially. One day, I came home and found a note saying she was in love with someone else."

Faith swallowed hard and, without hesitation, reached out for Joshua's hand. "Few men would have that kind of reaction to their ex becoming a mother. That's very selfless of you."

A slight smile tugged on his lip. "It's what I felt, at the time. Sure, I wish she'd wanted children with me. If I hadn't chosen to walk away from my father and the position, maybe eventually we would have started a family, but I have to believe God has another plan for me."

When she realized she was practically holding his hand, she pulled it away with a jerk.

What was she doing here—with him? What had started as a casual conversation between them had gotten way too personal. She broke eye contact with him and focused her attention on the storm. "Have you heard any updated weather reports?"

"The last I heard they were predicting a light dusting. Let me check my phone real quick." He pulled the device from his jacket pocket.

When a draft moved from the laundry room into the kitchen, Faith reached for her cable-knit sweater hanging on the back of her chair.

Joshua looked up from his phone, concern washing over his face. "Well, that changed fast. It looks like we're under a blizzard warning."

"What?" She bolted toward the windows and yanked open all of the plantation shutters. Normally, she could see the inn from her house, but now it was a wall of white.

He walked toward the open shutters. "Apparently, the smaller system they predicted is going to pull in more moisture off the coast. It's almost like a nor'easter." Joshua wrung his hands. "It doesn't sound good."

Faith paced the floor. "I've got to get Bella." She grabbed her car keys off the counter.

"Neither one of us could see our hand in front of our face out there, Faith. You can't drive with zero visibility."

She opened her mouth to protest, but stopped when a loud crash sounded in the backyard. They ran to the other window. "Oh, my word, look at the size of the branch that just fell."

"Exactly my point—you shouldn't be on the road. Those winds are much too dangerous." Joshua carefully tried to remove the keys from her hand.

Her grip tightened. "I have to get my daughter. She's not safe."

"She's inside a church. It's a pretty good spot to be, if you ask me."

A shiver shook her body. The congregation had been trying to raise enough money for a new roof since last year. "No, it's the worst place. The roof is damaged and in dire need of repair—actually it should be replaced." She looked out toward the raging storm. "I need her here. It's my job to protect my daughter. I made a promise."

Joshua picked up his phone and handed it to Faith. "Why don't you call Joy's house? They might be home safe and snug by now."

She took the device and punched in Joy's home number. The phone dropped from her ear. "All circuits are busy."

"Try her cell."

When she did—nothing. No fast busy signal. No recording. Only silence. How would she know if Bella was safe? Tears soaked her lashes. "It's dead. I've got to go."

"No. I will. You take care of the casserole and I'll head to the church. If they're not there, I'll go over to Joy's and bring Bella home."

"I can't ask that of you. It's too risky."

He reached for his jacket. Sliding his right arm inside, he turned. "If you don't mind, I'll take your SUV. It will do much better in the snow than my sedan."

"Yes…of course. Are you sure you want to do this? I've driven in these kinds of conditions before." Faith didn't think either of them should be out there, but she wanted her daughter home.

"Write down the directions to Joy's place." He zipped his jacket as he waited.

She scurried toward the desk and scribbled the route on the notepad. "Thank you for doing this, Joshua."

"I'll try to call once I'm at the church." He plucked the piece of paper from her extended hand. "I'll help you get the food to the inn when I get back. Whatever you do, don't go outside."

She wasn't sure she could make that promise since she needed to check on the guests. Even though Mr. and Mrs. Watson were there, the inn and her guests were her responsibility.

At the door, Joshua turned with a questioning eye. "Stay put, okay?"

She gave a slight nod. "Please, be careful."

Joshua opened the door and Mother Nature's fury burst inside the room. Icy air filled Faith's lungs as the papers scattered on the kitchen table were caught in a whirlwind. After a struggle, he pulled the door closed behind him.

Alone in the house now, she watched the howling wind, which was hypnotic. When another limb snapped outside, she walked to the window in search of headlights. A barricade of white surrounding the house made it impossible to see a thing. She moved toward the desk and opened the top drawer. Slipping down into the chair, she reached for something she hadn't touched since Chris's death…her Bible.

An hour and a half later, she pulled the casserole out from the oven. She hoped it was done— the power had flickered several times while the dish was inside. She paced the floor, unable to stand being alone in the house. Constant glances at the kitchen wall clock did nothing but make her realize how long Joshua had been gone. Against Joshua's advice, Faith bundled herself into her snowsuit and worked her way to the inn. A few gusts of wind nearly knocked her to the ground. She carried what she could of the food, and Mr. Watson went to retrieve the bread and the homemade brownies.

"I don't think I've ever seen it this bad," Mrs.

Watson said as she poured Faith a cup of coffee. The fireplace in the lounge area emitted an orange glow, a sharp contrast to the snow piling up outside.

"Are you okay, dear?"

Faith fingered her matted hair as they sat by the crackling fire. "I just wish the phones were working. Not knowing is making me crazy."

"Relax, dear. The Lord will look after them."

"But it's my job to look after Bella. I promised Chris before he died." Tears slid down her cheeks. "I feel so helpless and alone."

"You're never alone when you put your trust in Him. Chris was strong in his faith, and you must be, too." The older woman reached for her hand. "I know after his death you turned away from God, but He's never left your side."

Faith sighed, feeling uncomfortable at the direction this conversation was taking. But maybe it was time to face the truth. Horrible things did happen to good people, but it was not God's way of punishing anyone.

"He wants to walk with you, dear, and bring you out even stronger on the other side."

Faith knew this. She and Chris were always guided by the word of God. "Thank you. I know you're right. It's just taken me a while to realize it again."

"Chris has been gone for a number of years. It's time you move on with your life."

After Faith's grandmother had died, Mrs. Watson, her grandmother's best friend, had filled a void in her life. She was like a second grandmother to her. "I don't know if I can." Faith wept.

"Do you want to know what I've been thinking?" Mrs. Watson asked.

Faith nodded. "Sure."

"I hope I'm not being out of line, but you're like my own child—what about Joshua?" A hint of a smile crossed Mrs. Watson's narrow lips.

"What about him?" Faith wasn't ready to go down this road with her. She took a deep breath and prepared herself.

"It's apparent he's quite taken with you. And, if you were honest with yourself, I think you might be a little attracted to him, too."

As much as she didn't want to admit it, Mrs. Watson was right. She did find him handsome, and he'd shown nothing but concern for her and Bella since he'd arrived at Whispering Slopes. And now, who knew what kind of danger he could be in, trying to bring her daughter home. But none of it mattered, not when they both wanted the inn. "There's no chance for us." Her stomach soured by her words.

"Why not, dear?"

"He's here for the auction. With all of his money, he'll make the highest bid, and Chris's dream and mine will die."

"Maybe it's time for a new dream." Mrs. Watson squeezed Faith's hand. "What if God brought Joshua to Whispering Slopes to give you a new beginning?"

The woman was being absurd. "I highly doubt it."

"This could be your opportunity to build a new life with someone and find a father for Bella. You could finally regain the sense of security you long for."

Faith knew Mrs. Watson meant well, but she was way off. "If God brought Mr. Carlson here, it's to steal my dream. That's it—nothing more."

"You're not forsaking Chris's memory by moving forward. It's what he'd want."

When she and Chris had talked about the risks that came with his job, Faith had never wanted to face the possibility that each time he left for work, it could be the last time she saw him. He had needed to know she wouldn't wallow in grief for the rest of her life if the worst happened, but she'd just listened without assuring him. He wanted a promise she'd never been able to give him. She'd only vowed she'd take care of their daughter by providing a safe and secure future. "A little girl needs a daddy. If something were to happen to me, I want to know she'll be okay." The memory of his words made her blood run cold.

"Just think about it, dear. I'm going to get the guests some coffee and dessert."

Faith rose from her chair and walked toward the windows. Was Mrs. Watson right? Was she going against Chris's wishes? She jumped when her cell phone chirped. Without looking at the screen, she answered. "Hello?"

"It's Joshua. I've got our girl and we're on the way home."

The call disconnected, but his words lingered. *Our girl. Home.* As much as she wanted to believe Mrs. Watson about moving on, Joshua's comment sprung her back to reality. Bella was her girl and the Black Bear was their home. There wasn't room for outsiders.

An hour later, Joshua, Faith and Bella sat huddled by the fireplace at the inn, sipping hot chocolate topped with whipped cream. The fierce blizzard continued to rage outside. Despite the storm, a feeling of comfort washed over Joshua. It reminded him of his mother.

"You should have seen Mr. Joshua driving through the storm, Mommy. He was like a superhero." Bella had chattered nonstop since he'd brought her back to the safety of her mother's arms.

"She's great for a man's ego." Joshua winked at Faith.

"You couldn't even see the road. Oh, and he had to get out of the car twice to move huge branches out of the way. He's strong."

Faith fixated a gaze on him. There was something different. She actually seemed more tense than usual—if it were possible.

"Thank you for bringing Bella home safe." Her lips pursed.

Yep—something was up with her. Her daughter was her world. He'd thought she'd be over the moon when he brought her home. "This is where she belongs."

His own words rang true. Bella belonged here, at the home where her mother and aunt were raised. But he couldn't sacrifice his own mother's dream.

Bella squirmed from her chair and climbed into his lap. "It was like our own adventure, wasn't it?"

Around this child, he felt as though there wasn't anything in the world he couldn't accomplish, no matter what his ex-wife or father thought of him. "How about we have a little less adventure for a while? I don't think I can take much more excitement." He tickled Bella's side.

Bella wiggled free. "I'm going to go tell Mr. Watson all about it."

She took off skipping across the room and straight to the lobby.

The room went dark, but then the lights flickered on again.

Faith avoided eye contact with him and kept her gaze on the window. "If this snow keeps up, it's only a matter of time before we lose power."

"Does the inn have a generator?"

She nodded. "Yes. Thankfully, we have that, along with a stockpile of candles and flashlights. Of course, they're stored down in the cellar, which isn't a place you want to venture to in the dark."

When the lights sputtered again, Joshua pushed himself out of his chair. "Maybe we should go downstairs and get the supplies now, so we're not fumbling in the dark."

"My thoughts exactly." Faith rose and cleared away the mugs. "I'll check with Mrs. Watson to see if there's anything else she might need."

Ten minutes later, downstairs in the musty basement, they were digging through boxes thick with dust. Gurgles of water sounded from the pipes overhead. A sound all too familiar from his childhood stirred up memories he'd much rather forget.

Joshua couldn't help but sneak peeks at Faith to see if the tense look had faded from her face. Nope—still there.

"Are you upset about something? Bella's safe. I thought you'd be happy." He lifted a box from a stack and placed it on the ground.

"What makes you ask that?" She pulled her sweater down over her slim hips.

Something was on her mind. It was obvious. "When I left your house to get Bella, you seemed fine, concerned for her safety, of course, but now—I don't know…you seem mad at me. I'd like to know what I've done."

"It's nothing…just—"

"What? Please tell me."

She fingered the gold locket around her neck. "It's Bella."

"What about her?"

"She's getting too attached to you."

He released a heavy breath. "Is that it? I thought I'd done something wrong."

Faith paced the floor with her arms wrapped tightly around her waist. "You did—you are. You're letting her believe some fantasy you could possibly be her father."

"Seriously? How so? Really… I'd like to know." This was crazy. She'd seemed okay with him taking Bella to the father-daughter dance last night. Did she have a change of heart about it? Well, it was a little late for that.

"You said 'our girl.'"

He raked his fingers through his hair. This conversation was becoming more bizarre. "What on earth are you talking about?"

"When you found Bella and you called to tell me—you said, 'I found our girl' and you were bringing her home...like our home was yours, too."

"Whoa, wait a minute. After driving in those horrible conditions, my adrenaline was pumped up. I was excited and relieved to have found her safe. That's all it was. Believe me—I don't think Bella belongs to me...to us. She's a sweet little girl who I happen to enjoy being around—that's it!" He turned and resumed going through the box on the floor.

She stepped closer. "You have to understand. I've got to protect Bella from getting hurt, once you leave."

She really didn't understand. After the auction, Whispering Slopes would become his home. Perhaps it was some kind of defense mechanism. Who knew? One thing he was certain of—he wasn't going to be accused of leading on little Bella. He wouldn't hurt her for the world. But then his gut wrenched when he pictured her packing up her room.

He stood and stepped toward her. "I get it. But does this mean you don't want me at her birthday party next Saturday?"

Her forehead wrinkled. "She'd be crushed. You were the first person she put on the list."

"Fine—can we just drop this conversation before the power goes out?"

Ten minutes later, they'd put their differences aside, at least for now. Joshua filled a box with lanterns for the guests.

Faith opened a red storage container. "This box is full of candles."

Joshua rushed to her side. "Here, let me take that."

"I never knew there was so much stuff stored down here." She scanned the room, which appeared to cover the entire length of the inn. "Do you think all of those belong to your father?" She pointed to stacks of boxes on the far side of the room. "I know they aren't mine or the employees'."

Joshua's curiosity got the best of him. He headed across the room. Cobwebs tickling his face, he bent down to open the first box he came upon. Carefully, he peeled back the packaging tape. "It looks like this one is full of photo albums." He flipped through the pages covered with a clear plastic sheet protector. Inside, there were pictures of people he didn't recognize. He tucked the book back inside the box and pulled out another.

The sound of Faith's shoes tapping on the cement floor echoed as she approached. "Do you recognize anything?"

He opened the album and saw photos of his father as a child. In most of the pictures, he posed with another, much-younger-looking boy. "This is my father, but I don't know who the other child is."

She peered over his shoulder. "Maybe he's a cousin or neighborhood friend?"

"Could be." As he continued to study the young boy, he realized he had his father's eyes. He gently unpeeled the plastic and pulled the photo from the cardboard backing. Turning it over, he read the scribbled writing on the back. *Jimmy and RC four months before Jimmy's death.*

"Whoever this other boy is, he apparently died a few months after this photo was taken." Joshua scratched the side of his face.

"How sad."

Yes. But who was Jimmy? "I'm sure my father stored these boxes here, but why?"

Faith shrugged her shoulder slightly. "Maybe he didn't want anyone to see the contents or maybe he just doesn't have the room in his own house."

His father's house was a cold mansion capable of storing a million boxes. There was more to it. "Would you mind if I take a few of these boxes up to my room?"

"Of course not. Let's get the flashlights and candles upstairs first, and then I'll help you with the others."

Joshua headed back to the other side of the room and grabbed two boxes. What else was tucked away in this secret storage space? Could the contents inside these cardboard containers give him the answer to a question he'd carried since childhood?

Chapter Twelve

After the storm had moved out late Sunday night, all of Whispering Slopes had been snowed in for almost thirty-six hours. But in the mountains, people were resilient. By early Tuesday morning, everything was business as usual.

Faith glanced toward the open door in her office. Once again, she spotted the two men in dark pin-striped suits walking around the lobby as though they were looking for something, or maybe someone. They each carried a leather portfolio. What were they writing as they appeared to scope out their surroundings? She'd seen them wandering around the lounge earlier, pointing and whispering. Something didn't feel right.

When they exited the front door, she pushed herself away from her desk. Whenever she wanted to know something pertaining to the inn, she knew exactly who to ask, so she went in search of Mrs. Watson.

Expansive floor-to-ceiling windows inside the dining room provided a picturesque view of the snow-covered grounds. A family of deer trekked across the icy grounds, leaving behind their footprints glistening in the morning sun. Faith's heart fluttered. This was why she loved this land. She wouldn't allow Joshua to swoop in and take all of this away from her. She'd never let it go.

As she scanned the room, she spied a couple of the guests sitting at a large circular table situated in the middle of the room. They laughed as they sipped their coffee and nibbled on the croissants drizzled with chocolate, Faith's favorite. Mrs. Watson had picked up several dozen at the bakery this morning. After she caught up with Mrs. Watson, she'd finish some of the bookkeeping and head home to lend a hand to Joshua. Last night, he'd mentioned his plans to hit the slopes early this morning and then be at her house around 10:00 a.m. to begin preparing lunch.

Finding no sign of Mrs. Watson, she turned around. Her eyes landed on a striking redhead sitting in a leather club chair at the far corner of the room. Dressed in a black pencil skirt and an off-white sweater, the woman scribbled on a notepad resting on her lap, her never-ending legs crossed at the ankles. She paused and directed her focus to the bar area and then wrote some more. What was everyone writing today?

"There you are."

Startled by the voice, she turned toward the entryway. "Good morning, Mrs. Watson. I've been looking for you."

"Well, here I am. I'd been by your office, but it was empty. I thought maybe you'd decided to go skiing this morning—perhaps with Joshua?" She flashed a grin and winked. "He's such a nice young man. And quite handsome...don't you think?"

Faith couldn't argue with Mrs. Watson's observation. Joshua was extremely good-looking, something she found harder to ignore each day he showed up in her kitchen. What made him even more attractive was the kind and gentle way he treated Bella. But no matter how nice he was to look at, she knew she had to keep her distance and stay focused on her goal.

"Hello?" Mrs. Watson waved her hand in front of Faith's face.

"I'm sorry. What did you say?"

"Joshua...isn't he handsome?"

"Uh...yes—I don't know." She shook her head as if trying to get a housefly away from her face. "I wanted to ask you about those men in suits who I saw walking around the inn. Did you see them?"

Mrs. Watson ran her hands down the front of her apron speckled with tiny daisies. "Yes, I did. I even answered some of their questions."

Faith's throat constricted as she tried to swallow. "What were they asking you?"

"They asked about our occupancy rate, if our guests come from out of state. You know those types of questions."

"No, I don't know. Why would these strangers be asking questions about my inn—I mean, the inn?"

Mrs. Watson placed her hand on Faith's forearm. "They're investors, dear. My guess is they plan to bid at the auction, too."

Her words caused the room to spin. Faith stepped back to a nearby chair and collapsed into the cushioned back. She'd been so concerned about Joshua, focusing all her anger toward him and his desire for the inn that she'd failed to realize he wouldn't be the only competition. Why had she been so foolish? She leaned forward, resting her elbows on her knees and raked her fingers through her hair.

"I'm sorry, Faith. I thought you'd known there'd be others interested in the property."

She lifted up her head and pushed her hair

away from her face. "Is she an investor, too?" Faith pointed toward the redhead in the corner of the room.

"No, you don't have to worry about her. She's here to see Joshua." Both women looked in her direction before Mrs. Watson turned her gaze back on Faith. "See, you need to get out and spend some time with him because it looks as though you might have a little competition." She smiled and strolled out of the room.

Faith couldn't help but sneak quick glances at the woman waiting to see Joshua. Was her visit business or pleasure? The way she was dressed, it appeared to be business. Could it be about the inn? Her stomach quivered at the thought of their meeting being a personal one. But why would she care? Was the stunning woman his girlfriend? He'd never talked about being in a relationship, but then again, with her barriers up, when would he ever have had an opportunity? It couldn't be his ex-wife, could it?

She pushed herself out of the chair when she made the decision to find out the answers herself. After all, she was the manager here and her job was to meet and greet the guests. There was nothing at all wrong with sitting down to chat.

As she walked across the room, she noticed how focused the woman was on whatever she was writing. Faith clasped her hands behind her back and leaned in. "Hello, there. Welcome to the Black Bear Inn."

The woman stood and placed her notepad on her chair. She extended her hand. "Thank you. I'm Melissa Ferguson."

Faith took notice of Melissa's firm handshake. "My name is Faith Brennan. I'm the manager here. I make a point of greeting newcomers. Can I get you a cup of coffee or something else?"

"Coffee sounds great. This number crunching is putting me to sleep." She flashed an overly white smile.

"Why don't you have a seat over by the window? You can enjoy the view and I'll be right back." Faith headed to the bar and grabbed two mugs and the coffeepot. She couldn't help wondering if she was crunching numbers in preparation for the auction. How many more people would she be up against? Using all of the insurance money hadn't been part of her original plan, but if that was what she had to do, she had no other choice. There was no way she'd allow these outsiders to waltz in and take what belonged to her. They had no idea what it was like to live and work in this community. They'd never appreciate it as much as she did.

"Here you go." She poured the hot beverage for Melissa and then one for herself. "So tell me, do you plan to stay at the inn as our guest?"

Melissa shifted in her chair before answering. "Well, I guess that remains to be seen. I have to address a personal misunderstanding first." Her brow arched. "Wait a minute—Faith…you're the woman who's trying to take the inn away from Joshua, aren't you?"

This was bad—and totally unfair. She wasn't expecting this woman to know more about her. Had Joshua been talking about her? "Excuse me?"

Melissa's false eyelashes were like black woolly caterpillars. "Joshua told me you were his main competition."

"And you are?" Faith didn't trust this woman.

"Let's just say he and I are old friends. We've always been there for each other, ever since high school. I came in from DC to ensure he gets what he wants." She strummed her bright red acrylic nails on the table, producing an annoying click. "As long as I've known him, he's always gotten what he wanted."

Faith had a feeling Melissa was the type of person who always got what she wanted. It seemed to her, what Melissa wanted was Joshua. Funny…she really didn't seem like the type of person Joshua would be friends with.

"Melissa!"

Both women jumped at the authoritative tone echoing across the dining room.

Melissa was the first to leap to her feet as Joshua approached at a rapid pace…his face tomato red.

Faith stayed in her seat to observe the interaction. Her instinct told her she should leave, but she was dying to see what this was all about.

"I'm sorry, Faith, but can you excuse us? We have a few things to discuss."

Rats.

Joshua placed his hand on Melissa's lower back and guided her toward the door of his room. Faith kept her eye on them until they were gone. She had no idea what was going on between those two, but it was obvious Joshua didn't appreciate her visit to the inn. Her gaze turned to the window and she released a heavy sigh. Was Melissa right? Did Joshua always get what he wanted? In a little over a week, she'd find out.

The slam from the door jarred the Bob Timberlake painting hanging in Joshua's room. He spun around to face his unwanted guest. "I don't know what you were talking about with Faith, but I want to know everything—now!"

Melissa's eyes locked with his. Her face flushed.

"Well?" He had zero patience right now. Seeing her sitting with Faith had been the last thing he'd expected.

After carefully examining her fingernails, she dropped her hands to her side and stepped closer. "Come on, Joshua. Why are you so angry?" She reached her hand out toward him, but he stepped back to avoid contact.

"You don't work for me any longer, so I'm not sure why you're here." If she planned to ask for her job back, he wasn't going to oblige her.

She let out a nervous laugh and her eyelashes fluttered. "I know, silly. I didn't come with hopes of being your attorney again. You fired me and I understand why."

What? The Melissa he knew would never take rejection this easy, especially when it came to business. She was referred to as the "shark" in the legal community. Something was definitely up. "Spill it. We've known each other too long for me not to know you've got some crazy idea in your head."

"That's just it."

"What's it? What on earth are you talking about?"

Her gaze fixated on him. "All these years, our timing has always been off."

His mind raced in search of an answer. Where she was headed? Then his stomach twisted. "Don't even go there, Melissa. There's never been a timing issue for us. You were on my payroll, working as my attorney—nothing more."

"No! Don't you see? We've always had obstacles when it came to our relationship. You went away to college and then you married my best friend. Then I came to work for you, but now, there's nothing."

"You just hit the nail on the head. There isn't anything between us...no obstacles, no timing issues—nothing. I've never had those kinds of feelings for you." He swallowed hard when her expression went blank. He knew his words stung, but from experience, he knew shooting straight from the hip was the best way to handle her. "We had a couple of dates in high school—as friends."

"It was more...so much more." She spoke with a tight jaw. "Don't you remember the night of the senior class picnic—we kissed."

The kiss. He'd completely forgotten about it. As soon as he'd done it, he'd regretted it, but he never imagined it to be anything memorable. "We were kids. I didn't know what I was doing." He raked his hand over his face. "I guess I thought that's what I was supposed to do. I'd forgotten all about it until you mentioned it just now."

Melissa cleared her throat. "Oh—ah... I see."

She shuffled at a brisk pace to the door. Clutching the knob, she turned. She inhaled a slow and steady breath and, her eyes like daggers, said, "I never forgot."

When the door shut behind her, an unsettling feeling took hold of Joshua. Her carefully controlled tone signaled a warning this wouldn't be the last he'd see of Melissa.

Friday evening, Joshua showered and dressed in tan corduroy pants and a waist-length dark brown leather coat. He grabbed Bella's birthday gift off the desk in his room and headed to the community center. Outside, a light snow fell as a gusty wind whipped tiny pellets of ice against his cheeks. He'd need to invest in a few wool scarves to survive the winters around here. He climbed inside his car and buckled his seat belt. His gaze flicked to the front of the inn and he caught sight of the cozy cottage adjacent to the property—Faith and Bella's house. His stomach lurched. When all was said and done, was he really the type of businessman who'd put someone out of their home? He shook off the negative thoughts and allowed his mother to enter his mind. She'd help him figure out what to do.

Minutes later, he zipped into a parking spot at the Whispering Slopes Community Center. Tiny white lights twinkled across the top and sides of the small brick building. A warm and welcoming establishment for the townspeople to gather—his mother would have loved it.

He'd been excited to see Bella. The week had been busy, so he'd seen little of her sweet face. The girl had taken up residency in his heart and filled a void he never knew existed. He hadn't seen Faith, either, over the past several days. Since Melissa's unwelcome visit, each time he went to Faith's house to cook meals for the inn, she seemed conveniently gone. Was she avoiding him? At the inn, her office door, which had usually been open for visitors, stayed closed.

He'd arrived a little early and settled into a corner table. A bustling waitstaff carried plates of children's favorite foods to a long buffet table. The aroma of chicken fingers and hot dogs made him realize how hungry he was—he hadn't eaten since lunch. The sounds of children giggling as they wandered into the banquet hall accompanied by their parents filled the air. There was no sign of Bella or Faith.

Although he'd been preoccupied for most of the week with auction business and cooking, Faith had been in the forefront of his mind. He hoped tonight he could learn if she'd been deliberately avoiding him. Had Melissa said something to upset her? He was about to find out.

His gaze landed on her just then. Standing alone in the doorway, dressed in a winter-white turtleneck sweater and white pants, Faith looked more beautiful than ever. He wished she didn't. Her hair hung loose, cascading over her shoulders. Her almond-shaped eyes connected with his from across the room and she smiled. As she glided across the floor toward him, Joshua tried to ignore his racing pulse.

He stood and reached for her hand. A few seconds passed as he inhaled the familiar scent and they exchanged darted glances. "You look amazing tonight. White's definitely your color—you're radiant." When her eyes avoided his, he knew his compliment had made her feel uncomfortable. "I'm sorry. I didn't mean to embarrass you."

She turned her gaze in his direction. "No—you didn't. Thank you for coming, Joshua. It means the world to Bella." Her cheeks flushed.

"I don't think I could ever say no to her." His stomach twisted. Would Bella still feel the same about him after the auction? Or would she look at him as the mean old man who stole her home? By this time next week, he'd have his answer.

Faith laughed. "You're in trouble now."

He took a quick scope of the room. "Where is the guest of honor?"

"She's with Joy. They went to pick up her

friend, Missy. Her parents had other plans tonight." She threw a glance over her shoulder at the sound of a large crowd entering the room. "I better go and greet the guests."

Joshua offered a weak smile. Of course, she was the hostess, but he had to admit to being a bit disappointed not to have some alone time with Faith.

She studied him for a moment. "I'm sorry. I know you don't really know any of these people. It's rude of me to just abandon you. I'll go say hi to everyone and come back—if you want some company."

"That would be nice."

A smile parted her lips as she scurried toward the crowd huddled around a table, admiring the large Snoopy birthday cake. Bunches of oversize balloons with characters from a popular comic were tied to each table.

For his seventh birthday, his mother had thrown him a superhero-themed party. All of his friends dressed as their favorite hero—and his mom had gotten in on the action, too. His father had been a no-show, which was his modus operandi throughout his childhood. But like Bella, he'd had the perfect mother.

Joshua's thoughts drifted to Bella. Being raised by a single mother wasn't much different from what he'd experienced. With his father always absent for family functions, it was as though his own mother was single. He prayed not having a father figure in her life wouldn't leave an ever-present void in Bella's life, like the void in his.

For the next ten minutes, Joshua observed Faith as she gracefully greeted the parents and children who'd come to celebrate her daughter's sixth birthday. Her complexion glowed like fresh summer peaches under the recessed lighting. She was the perfect hostess. Many of her qualities reminded him of his mother. A thickness formed in his throat as he realized he was alone in the world. He no longer had someone in his life to love—or someone who loved him.

But when Faith approached his table, her pleasant smile had faded.

Maybe she'd changed her mind about sitting with him. With the auction a week away, tensions between them were bound to grow, yet for some reason, sitting across from this striking woman, the auction was the last thing on his mind.

"Is everything okay?"

"Yes—well, not really. Joy just called, and her car won't start. She's waiting on the auto club to come and check out the problem." She released a long sigh. "I guess I better make an announcement so Bella's guests know what's going on."

Faith informed the partygoers the guest of honor would be delayed. Inviting them to help themselves to food and drinks, she set the microphone back onto the podium and returned to Joshua's table.

"Please have a seat." Had he purposely slid it a little closer to his own? He loved being around Bella, but he was grateful for some time alone with Faith. He'd wanted to talk to her about Melissa. "We haven't seen each other in a few days."

She nodded. "Yes, I guess we've both been busy."

"I've wanted to apologize for anything Melissa might have said or done to upset you." At the mention of Melissa's name, he noticed Faith's shoulders go tense as she squirmed in her seat.

"I'm not sure what you're referring to. She didn't say anything other than the fact the two of you were old friends and she'd come to Whispering Slopes on personal business." Her left brow arched. "Why would you think anything she said might have upset me? She's of no concern to me."

"Melissa was my attorney—up until recently. I had some trust issues with her and had to let her go. She's not taking it well." He knew it wasn't the entire truth, but there was no need to share with Faith what had transpired up in his room. He'd hoped this would be the last he heard from Melissa, but somehow he doubted it.

"Well, it's really none of my business."

Ten minutes later, her eyes turned toward the front door. "If you'll excuse me, my daughter and sister just arrived." She pushed herself away from the table and, with her shoulders stiff, made her way to her family.

Joshua watched as Bella raced to her mother. The stoic look painted on Faith's face while she sat with him moments earlier vanished as soon as her daughter was in her arms. He turned away when his phone chirped. He glanced down at the device sitting on the table. His mouth dropped open when he saw a text message from Melissa.

The inn will never be yours.

Chapter Thirteen

"My foot hurts, Mr. Joshua."

Bella's curls glistened under the fluorescent lights at Valley Memorial Hospital. Seeing her slip on the ice outside the inn late on Tuesday afternoon, he and Mrs. Watson had sprung into action. Thankfully, Bella hadn't hit her head, but her ankle had twisted like a stubborn ketchup lid. Faith had gone into town with Joy to run a few errands, so he and Mrs. Watson were keeping an eye on Bella. Joshua had volunteered to take her to the hospital and Mrs. Watson followed in her own car. Once at the hospital, the woman stayed for a few minutes before she had to get back to the inn.

"I know it's painful, sweetie," he said. "They should take you back soon for an X-ray."

Her curious blue eyes stared up at him. "What's an X-ray?" She squirmed on the love seat and leaned closer to him. Her eyes looked down and glimmered with fear. "Will it hurt?"

He flinched. *Hurt.* It wasn't always about physical pain. The hurt his father had bestowed jabbed deep, without his ever having laid a hand on his son. "Oh, no, it's only a picture of your foot. It's nothing."

A giggle rose from her throat. "Why do they want to take a picture of my foot?"

"To see if you have a broken bone."

She gripped his arm and blinked several times. "Winston from my class broke his arm. He said the doctor re-breaked it and it really hurt." Her eyes grew wide. "Are they going to do that to me?" She nuzzled closer. "I'm scared."

He cast his gaze upon the frightened child and his chest squeezed. Growing up without a father, she searched for comfort from a man she hardly knew. Joshua wouldn't be like his father and tell her to "man up, life is hard." Instead, he ran his hand across her forehead. "There's nothing to be afraid of, sweetie. I'll be right there with you. I won't let anyone hurt you."

Bella wiggled into his lap and looked up at him with teary eyes. "I wish you were my daddy, Mr. Joshua."

Unsure what to say, he narrowed his focus on the child as her wish crept deeper into his heart.

He glanced around the empty waiting room as voices echoed down the hall. If this was what it felt like, he wished he was her father, too.

His thoughts were interrupted when she released a heavy sigh. "I didn't know my daddy, but I still miss him."

Joshua's heart broke for the child. "I know you do." He spoke in a quiet tone.

She remained silent for a moment and then gave a slight shrug of her shoulders. "He's in Heaven now, so he can always see me."

They both turned to the sound of heels clicking down the tile floors.

"Bella—baby, what happened?" Faith dashed inside, concern spilling over her face. Joy, who was with her, looked just as frightened.

As Faith leaned toward him, Joshua inhaled the scent of lavender. She threw her arms around her daughter's neck, smothering her cheeks with kisses.

"Mommy, you're getting me all wet." With the palm of her hand, she wiped off her face. "I slipped on the ice, but it's okay, Mr. Joshua's been taking care of me. Mrs. Watson came, too, but she had to leave," Bella announced.

Heat crept up his neck when Faith looked at him and smiled. "Thank you for bringing Bella to the hospital and staying with her. When Mr. Watson called my cell, Joy and I got here as fast as we could." Her eyes looked away. "You don't have to stay."

Bella jerked in his lap. "No! He said he'd stay with me." Her breath quivered as she looked into his eyes. "You promised, Mr. Joshua."

He nodded. "You're right. I did. I'm not going anywhere."

She let out a heavy sigh. "After they re-break my foot, maybe Mr. Joshua can come over for Sunday dinner."

Joshua's stomach twisted. The auction was on Saturday. Sunday morning, their lives would be changed forever.

"Re-break? What?" Faith's eyes widened as she first looked at Joy and then back to Joshua.

He slid Bella off his lap and onto the love seat. "Joy, do you mind if Faith and I go down to the cafeteria for some coffee? The nurse said it'll be at least an hour before they can get her back into X-ray." Joshua scanned his watch. "That was over thirty minutes ago."

Faith studied him as he stood up. "I could sure use some caffeine. Is that okay, Joy?"

Her sister slid into the seat next to Bella. "Sure, just bring me back a cup—black, please."

Joshua placed his hand on the small of Faith's back and guided her down the corridor. The ER doors whooshed open behind them, reminding him of her anxiety when it came to hospitals. "Are you okay?"

"Yes, I'm fine."

Her eyes peeled to the Exit sign told him otherwise.

Once inside the cafeteria, the aroma of unpalatable foods and hand sanitizer turned Joshua's stomach. Doctors dressed in scrubs buzzed around the room, grabbing a quick cup of coffee before it was time to move on to their next patient. An elderly man with snow-white hair sat at the corner table with his head in his hands. His shoulders quivered. A younger man patted him on the back. Were they father and son? Had the wife and mother been admitted into one of the rooms inside the hospital? Joshua shook off thoughts of his own mother.

"Let's take a seat by the window. We can watch the snow flurries." His pulse quickened at the thought of spending a few minutes alone with Faith. What was it about her? He'd been fighting these feelings surfacing whenever she was present. But why? There was no chance of a future for them. He'd never be able to grant Bella her wish. That only happened in fairy tales, like the ones his mother read to him as a child.

With a gentle hand on her arm, he guided her toward the round table with a wood-veneer top and a cast-iron base. Salt and pepper shakers sat in the middle, along with a silver napkin holder.

Faith took a seat and wrapped her arms around her chest.

"If you're too cold next to the window, we can move." Caught off guard by his intense need to protect her, he pointed toward a table across the room.

Faith shook her head and gazed out the window. "This is fine. I like to watch the snow falling."

Warmth traveled through Joshua's body. He enjoyed it, too. "I'll get us some coffee. That'll warm you up." He winked and, with a turn, headed toward the beverage station.

Within minutes, they were both clutching their steaming disposable cups.

"Do you really think they'll have to re-break her foot?"

He shook his head. "Nah, some classmate was trying to sound tough in front of his friends. It's probably only a sprain. There didn't appear to be much swelling."

A smile slid across her lips. "Thank you. That makes me feel better." She ran her finger along the top of her cup. "It's no wonder Bella thinks of you as her superhero. This is the third time since you've arrived in Whispering Slopes you've come to her rescue." Her cheeks flushed. "Mine, too, actually."

His chest grew heavy at her words—after all, his future plans to develop the Black Bear Inn made him the bad guy. He couldn't help wondering if there was a way they could each get what they wanted. Of course, he knew that was impossible. They both wanted ownership of the inn. He squeezed his eyes shut. "I'm afraid you and Bella will feel differently after the auction."

Faith remained silent. He couldn't blame her. What could she say?

Seconds later, she drew in a deep breath and exhaled. "Let's change the subject."

Fine by him.

"I've wanted to say thank-you, but the time hasn't ever seemed right."

"Thank me?" He couldn't imagine what for. Once he gained ownership of the Black Bear and the expansion project began, she'd be anything but grateful.

"Yes, you made me realize how wrong I've been."

His eyes narrowed. "About what?"

She hesitated and drew in a breath. "Remember the day I got angry about Bella coming into your room?"

Boy, did he ever. Her face lit up like a red-hot chili pepper. "Yes, I do."

"I'd overheard her telling you about the photographs of her father…or should I say lack of pictures."

He nodded. "Go on."

She clasped her hands together and rested them on the table. "I know you must have thought I was a horrible person."

"I could never think that about you." Especially lately, when thoughts of her consumed his mind from the moment he woke up each day.

"No, it's true. I was so busy protecting my own feelings I couldn't see I was depriving Bella of her father's memory." She inhaled a deep breath and released it. "I was wrong, so thank you."

He kept his attention focused on Faith and reached across the table for her hand. "Don't blame yourself. You did what you had to do to survive, Faith." When she gave his hand a squeeze his heart thumped at the possibilities. What was happening here?

A hint of a smile caused slight dimples to root in her cheeks. "After that day, Bella and I spent an evening going through boxes of old pictures. You should have seen how excited she was. Watching her get to know her father through captured moments in time was one of the greatest joys in my life."

Relief washed over him as he leaned back into his chair. Now this sweet child could begin to know her daddy. This made him happy, but at the same time, an intense longing took hold. The unconditional love of a child had to be the greatest feeling in the world. "I'm happy things worked out for you." He swallowed the lump clogging his throat. "Really, Faith, I couldn't be happier."

"Things turned out better than I'd imagined and I owe it all to you, a complete stranger."

His shoulders slumped. "Do you still think of me that way?"

She hesitated for a moment and searched his eyes. "No, not after all the time we've spent together, but you were, then. You've changed my life—and my daughter's. I'll be forever grateful."

His chest grew tight. *Grateful.* Would she still feel the same way when he'd have to ask her and Bella to pack their bags? Suddenly, the cup of coffee he'd been enjoying turned bitter on his tongue.

Wednesday morning, Faith propped her king-size pillow behind Bella's back. Her daughter always liked to sleep in her mother's bed when she wasn't feeling well. "You heard the doctor, you have a slight sprain. He wants to you stay off your leg for today."

Bella flung her shoulders back against the pillow. "But my ankle doesn't hurt anymore. Besides, I want to see Mr. Joshua when he comes over to cook."

"Don't you want to go to the pizza party at school tomorrow?" Faith bent down and opened the credenza underneath the TV in her bedroom. She had a large collection of DVDs, many of which she and Chris had watched together on their Saturday date nights. Her breath hitched. Now only Bella watched those movies. "So, what movie would you like to watch?"

"Oh, yeah… I forgot about the pizza party." A smile filled her face. "Do you think Mr. Joshua would come? We're allowed to invite anybody."

Faith's pulse surged at the mention of Joshua's name. "I doubt it." She placed her hands on her hips and turned toward the bed. "Now, what movie do you want?"

"Why won't he?"

Bella's attachment to Joshua was getting out of control. Sure, Faith appreciated everything he'd done for both her and Bella, but she had to protect her daughter's heart. Or was it her own heart she was protecting? "If you don't tell me what you want, you'll be sitting in here in silence."

Bella whistled and clapped her hands. "Plato, come and watch *Cinderella* with me."

Of course, she was obsessed with Cinderella—and Joshua.

With Bella resting, Faith did a little spot cleaning in the kitchen. Glancing at the clock, she realized Joshua would be by any minute to prepare lunch. From the moment she woke up this morning, thoughts of the auction and Joshua's good looks had consumed her mind. In three days, her fate would be sealed. Over the past several weeks, she'd tried to convince herself she could outbid Joshua or any investor, but who was she kidding? Yes, the insurance money was a large amount, but even with Joy's financial assistance, she couldn't release the nagging feeling that it just wasn't enough.

This morning, as she'd sipped her first cup of coffee, she'd finally decided to take her sister's advice. She'd tell Joshua about the dream she and Chris shared. She knew playing the sympathy card might be an unfair tactic, but what other choice did she have? It was obvious, especially the other day at the hospital, how Joshua seemed very protective when it came to Bella. Could it play to her advantage, as well?

Her stomach felt like an empty pit when she heard a car door slam. A few seconds later, a gentle knock signaled her guest had arrived.

The dream she'd had the night before where she and Joshua were married popped into her head. Now? Really? She raked her fingers through her wavy curls as she opened the door.

"Good morning." He stepped inside, removing his leather coat. He was dressed in jeans, his dark wavy hair barely touching the collar of his crisp white shirt. Her heart hammered inside her chest. She caught a whiff of a musky scent, triggering a memory of Chris. The smell of his aftershave had always made her feel safe. "So what's on the menu today?"

He placed three shopping bags on the kitchen table. "I thought I'd go with a taco bar."

Her stomach grumbled as the coffee churned inside. She hadn't had a chance to run up to the inn earlier to grab a bagel. Mrs. Watson had picked up several dozen for the guests. After making pancakes for Bella, her appetite had disappeared. "That sounds really good. I hope you got both crunchy and soft shells."

Joshua laughed as he pulled both kinds from the bag. "What's your preference?" He flashed a grin that made her knees buckle.

"I'm a crunchy gal—always have been."

"I love the soft shells. We sound like the perfect—"

Faith took notice of the smile quickly vanishing from Joshua's face when he'd realized what he was saying. It did seem like they were a perfect match, except when it came to their battle over the inn.

He cleared his throat. "Sorry, maybe a little bit of wishful thinking on my part, but I'll be completely honest—if it weren't for the Black Bear, I would have asked you on a date by now."

Faith's face warmed as her heart fluttered. A date? The two of them? "Look, Joshua, I owe you an apology. Ever since I learned your reasons for coming here, I've been a real jerk."

"That's a little harsh. Perhaps you haven't been Little Miss Sunshine, but I understand your reasons."

She closed her eyes and took a calming breath. "Can we sit down and talk for a minute?"

They each pulled a chair out from under the table and took a seat.

"Before Chris was killed in the fire, he and I had a plan."

Joshua leaned across the table and tenderly brushed her hair away from her face. "I'd like to hear it—if you want to talk about it."

"We planned to open an inn. It was his dream at first, but the more we talked about it, I became excited, too." She paused as the memory caused her eyes to prickle with tears. "It doesn't matter anymore."

"Of course it does. It's important to have dreams. Why would you say that?"

She looked down at her hands and picked her fingernail. "I know I'm not going to be the highest bidder at the auction. For weeks, I've tried to pretend it wasn't true. But the confidence I've displayed has been an act."

"I'm so sorry."

Faith shrugged her shoulders and looked at him. She was surprised by the sincerity emanating from his blue-ice eyes. "Oh, come on, you should be happy." She forced a laugh. "I'm the only other person planning to bid on the inn." She paused to steady her breathing. "If that's the case, you're a shoo-in now."

As soon as she spoke, she knew her tone was condescending and his face confirmed it.

"I didn't come here to steal your dream."

Her eyebrow arched. "Not on purpose at least."

"I wish you had shared this with me sooner."

She traced her finger along the tabletop, avoiding eye contact. "Joy wanted me to, but I didn't see any point."

Joshua ran his hand across his clean-shaven face. "All along, I thought the inn meant so much because it's where you grew up and it's your home now. But this—it changes everything."

She shook her head. "It doesn't change anything. You have your own reasons and I'm sure they matter just as much to you. It all comes down to money and the fact is you have more."

Joshua hesitated before turning toward her. "Whispering Slopes was my mother's favorite place on earth. Before she died, she asked me to never let it out of our family."

Faith turned and their eyes held. She knew his mother had meant the world to him. It was an endearing quality among others he seemed to possess. The last thing he'd ever want to do was not live up to a promise he'd made to her. "Then why would your father want to put it up for auction?"

He released a heavy breath. "My father is angry at me for quitting my job with his company. When I quit, I became a huge nothing to him."

"Maybe you're making a bigger deal out of this than it really is. Can't you talk to him?"

He ran his palms up and down the top of his thighs. "According to my father, if you're not a success in the business world, you don't matter. I quit, so I no longer matter in his life."

Faith could hear the pain in his voice. Did he believe this lie? Surely this was all a big misunderstanding. She rested her hand on his forearm. "You should talk to him. Maybe he'll change his mind about the auction."

"Trust me, the man will never change. I learned that many years ago." He turned and headed toward the stove to start sautéing the ground beef.

Faith watched as his shoulders were slumped in defeat. Surely his father wasn't that insensitive. Maybe she could call him and try to convince him the auction wasn't a good idea. But why would he care what she thought? She was just an employee and a tenant. As the smell of browning beef and onions filled the sunny kitchen, Faith started to worry. With the anger Joshua carried toward his father, he seemed more determined than ever to make sure he fulfilled his mother's wish.

But where would it leave her and Bella?

Chapter Fourteen

Early Friday morning, after a restless night of sleep, Joshua sprung from his bed at 5:00 a.m. He hadn't been able to get Faith and her late husband's dream out of his mind the previous night. After a great deal of prayer into the early morning hours, finally a sense of peace had filled his heart. Why hadn't he thought of this before? It was the perfect solution.

Of course, now he had to convince Faith. That might not be so easy.

He fired up his one-cup coffee maker and inhaled the invigorating aroma. As his beverage brewed, Joshua walked toward the sitting area and turned on the desk light. Easing himself into the chair, he fingered through some of the family photos he'd discovered in the basement of the inn. He'd racked his brain trying to figure out who this Jimmy fella was and what his relationship had been with his father. Why hadn't his name ever been mentioned? There were so many photos of the two of them together. He took one and slid it inside his wallet.

At six o'clock, dressed in gray slacks and a maroon cable sweater, he stood on Faith's front porch. He released a slow and steady breath of excitement and knocked gently on the door, in case Bella was still sleeping. Faith's beauty was revealed as she slowly opened the door. Her shiny caramel hair tumbled loosely over her shoulder and her skin radiated a pink hue. "You look beautiful this morning."

Her face flushed instantly. "Well, good morning to you, too." She smiled as she opened the door wider. "And thank you for the compliment." Her eyes quickly shot to the ground.

Feeling at home after weeks of Faith opening her kitchen to him, Joshua headed toward the coffeepot. He'd need a lot more caffeine in order to get breakfast cooked for the guests, as well as talk to Faith about his plan. He removed the pot from the burner, grabbed an oversize mug and turned to her. "Would you like some, too?"

"Oh, no—I'm supposed to be cutting back. I've been drinking this stuff since two o'clock this morning." She picked a loose thread on her white cardigan sweater.

"Couldn't sleep?"

"Not a wink. And you?"

He shook his head. "I think I counted every sheep in the state of Texas."

Faith laughed and slid into a chair at the kitchen table.

Joshua headed to the pantry and grabbed a bag of Vidalia onions. He walked to the table and glanced down at Faith. Her head dawdled. "Is my assistant petering out on me?"

Her body jerked and she pushed herself out of the chair. "No, I'm here to assist." She gave him a playful salute. "What's on the menu this morning?"

"One of my favorite dishes—farmer's casserole." He placed the onions on the counter and then retrieved a sack of potatoes.

Faith chuckled. "What? I've never heard of such a dish. What's in it?"

"You mean to tell me you grew up in the country and you've never heard of it?" Joshua grabbed the potato peeler and passed it to Faith. "Lots of potatoes—so you better start peeling, young lady." He opened the bag and poured all of them into a large bowl.

Her mouth dropped open. "All of these?"

"We've got an inn full of hungry guests— myself included."

Twenty minutes later, Faith was finished with

her assigned duty. Joshua grabbed the potatoes and began to dice them into chunks. "Once I make these into hash browns, all that's left to do is mix some eggs and evaporated milk, then layer in the ham and pepper jack cheese. Ideally, you'd like it to sit overnight, but we don't have time." When he was a child, his mother had made this dish on snowy winter mornings. He missed that special time with her. She'd always been so interested in the books he was reading, or what he thought his future held. He stared down at the cheesy goodness, wishing for just one more of those conversations.

"You okay?" Faith's eyebrows crunched.

He blinked twice. "Yeah. My mother used to make this dish. I always felt safe and protected when she cooked it. Strange—huh?"

"No, not at all. I feel the same way about fried chicken. My grandmother cooked it every Sunday, after church. Whenever I smell it frying now, I picture her hunkered over the stove, wearing her apron with little red cherries embroidered into the fabric."

Silence filled the room as they both took a trip down memory lane.

Faith cleared her throat. "The recipe sounds pretty easy." She snatched a piece of cheese. "Even I could make this."

"So, do you not like to cook or you're just not very good at it?"

"No, Joy got the cooking gene. But I love to clean up." She grabbed the now-empty pot that had held the potatoes and turned on the faucet.

With all of the ingredients in two large casserole dishes, Joshua placed them into the oven. "We'll be good to go in about forty-five minutes."

She walked to the desk and grabbed her phone. "Great, I'll shoot Mrs. Watson a message, so she can let the guests know."

Joshua watched Faith as she tucked a strand of hair behind her ears while writing the text. Every moment he spent with her, he found himself having these crazy thoughts of what it would be like to be married to her. After Jessica, he'd never imagined he'd have these feelings for someone again, but Faith was different. She'd ignited feelings he thought would never come alive again.

"Okay, that's done. Let's have a seat at the table." She placed her phone on the counter as they both eased into their chairs. "Thank you, Joshua."

He smiled. "Don't thank me until you try the casserole."

She fingered the cross around her neck, her eyes steady on his. "Not that. I really appreciate all the help you've given me over the past several weeks. Honestly, I don't know what I would have done if you hadn't offered your cooking expertise. You've been a lifesaver, truly, you have."

What she didn't realize was she and Bella had been his own lifesavers. When he'd first arrived at Whispering Slopes, his desire to get the inn was a selfish one. Sure, he wanted it for his mother, but really, his need to prove something to his father had played a part, as well. Now, after all this time had passed, he couldn't even remember exactly what he was trying to prove. All he knew was he wanted Faith to have the security she'd lost when Chris was killed.

Joshua rubbed his sweaty palms down his thighs. How could he get her to understand they could both have their dream? "I have an idea, but before you panic and think I've completely lost my mind, I'd like you to give it some consideration."

Her lips parted into a smile. "Okay, I'm listening."

"I know how much you love the inn, but I also know it means security for you and Bella. For me, owning the inn is a chance to carry out my mother's last wishes. Neither is more important than the other." His prayers had been answered last night when God had given him the solution. He swallowed hard with hopes his other prayer would be answered, as well. "Why can't we both have what we want?"

Her eyebrows squished together. "I'm not sure what you mean."

"You don't have enough money to bid on the property, or at least, you don't have as much as I do. And keep in mind, there could be other investors interested in the property."

She clasped her hands together and rested them on the table. "I guess it's been wishful thinking on my part that no one else would come to the auction and you'd suddenly realize you didn't want it." A half smile tugged at her mouth.

"Yeah, I guess I was kind of hoping for the same thing." He reached across the table, placing his hands over hers. It felt like coming home. "I have a plan—well, actually it was God's idea, I'm just the messenger."

"I'm listening." Her hands remained underneath his.

His shoulders relaxed. A few weeks ago, she would never have been open to hearing any plan. This was good. Excitement coursed through his body as he took a deep breath and slowly exhaled.

"What if we own the inn together?"

Her eyes blinked several times as his plan

filtered through her brain. She didn't move or say a word.

"Faith? Tell me what you're thinking."

"I don't understand." Her head tilted to one side.

Tired of playing things safe, he spoke freely. "I don't want to lose you—and Bella." This didn't sound right. He didn't have them in the first place. "Wait, that's not what I meant. I just... I want to continue spending time with you. If we move forward with you and me against one another, someone will lose. This might sound crazy, but I don't care. Since that first day I found you frantically searching for Bella, you've had my heart—both of you." There, he'd said it. The humming of the hot water tank in the corner of the laundry room filled the room. "Knowing what the inn means to you, there's no way I can take it away from you. But, it means a lot to me, too."

Faith's mouth opened, but no words were spoken.

"I'm sorry if this is all too much for you, but one thing we both know is no one is promised a tomorrow. Our life can change on a dime."

"You want to own the inn together?"

The truth. He wanted more than a business partnership. He longed for her to be his life partner. He'd keep that thought to himself, but he wasn't sure for how much longer. "Yes. Last night I prayed for a way. This is it. We can both have what we want."

"What about my home? How does it fit into your plans of expanding the inn into a larger resort?"

Joshua knew one of her biggest concerns was losing her home. He had an idea he'd been praying about, and it could be the perfect solution. "I want to turn the inn into a home for you and Bella. With a little remodeling, it'll be exactly like the house you and Joy grew up in."

She blinked and gulped air. "But where would the guests stay?"

"My plan is to build a bigger place, more like a resort hotel."

Faith tilted her neck from one side to the other. "My head is spinning."

"I know this is a lot to dump on you at once, but the auction will be here before we know it." He gave her hand a gentle squeeze. "I want to do this for you—for us."

She pulled her hand away. Tucking a strand of hair behind her ear, she smiled. "Let's do this." Her eyes glistened with tears.

Joshua's heart soared. Her three little words had made him the happiest he'd been in years.

The sounds of tiny feet tapping against the hardwood filled the room. Joshua turned to a vision that caused his heart to skip a beat. Bella tore into the room wearing her one-piece footie pajamas, her hair a wild wad of curls.

"Mommy, Mommy! Is it true? Is Mr. Joshua really buying the inn for us? Are we going to be a family?" She jumped up and down.

Joshua wiped the perspiration forming on his brow. He wasn't sure how Faith would receive her daughter's excitement. He definitely didn't want Faith to get scared and change her mind.

Bella jerked to a halt. "Sorry... I know I'm not supposed to listen when you're talking to someone."

Faith took Bella's hand and led her to the kitchen table. "Sit down for a second, sweetie." Mother and daughter both took seats. "Mr. Joshua and I are going into business together. We're going to own the inn, as a partnership. We're not getting married."

Bella turned her head and grinned at Joshua.

His heart puddled like a snow cone in August.

"So, you're staying in Whispering Slopes?"

He nodded. "Yes, I'll be here—"

Before he finished his sentence, she pounced from her chair and made a beeline toward him. She jumped into his lap, wrapping her tiny arms around his neck. "I knew you wouldn't leave us."

Joshua savored the moment of feeling loved and appreciated, something only his mother had made possible for him to experience as long as she'd lived. No more. When he scooped her up in his arms, he turned toward Faith. There were tears, but she was smiling, too. He gave her a wink and she nodded.

"No, Bella, I'm not leaving you—I never will."

His cell phone pinged, indicating a new message. He fished it from his pocket and glanced at the screen. A chill scuttled down his spine. He stared at the phone in disbelief.

"What is it, Joshua?"

He placed Bella back on the ground and squeezed his eyes closed. "It's a text from my father. He's here and he wants to talk with me."

Faith approached him. The scent of her perfume calmed his nerves for a moment.

"But I didn't think he planned to attend the auction."

"Me, neither." This wasn't good. Not at all. His father must have somehow gotten wind of his plan to bid on the inn. Could it have been Melissa? He knew his father was up to something, but what? "Can you keep an eye on the casseroles for me?"

She nodded. "I'll bring them to the house when they're ready. Oh, by the way, Mr. and

Mrs. Watson said they'd take care of lunch and dinner today, so you won't need to rush back."

Within five minutes, Joshua was trudging through the snow-packed grounds toward the inn. A sharp northerly wind cut into his face. Despite the cold, he was burning up inside. If his father had come to try and ruin his plans for a future in Whispering Slopes with Faith and Bella, he'd be in for a fight.

He climbed the front porch steps, leaving a trail of puddled wet snow. He hadn't seen his father or spoken with him since his mother's funeral. Exhaling a deep breath, he wiped his feet on the welcome mat, gripped the frosty doorknob and entered the inn.

Joshua scanned the foyer. His heart practically stopped when he spotted a man who resembled his father, near the check-in desk. But this man looked twenty years older. His hair, normally cut high and tight, was scraggly, with much more gray sprinkled in than he remembered. His posture, which had once been marine-like, now slumped as he leaned against the wall. He no longer looked like the powerful businessman he was. As Joshua approached him, he tried to shake off the fear his father had always evoked in him ever since his childhood, when his father would lock him in the basement for not getting straight A's on his report card, or punish him otherwise for only getting a base hit in baseball and not a home run.

Their eyes locked when his father lifted his head. His once-lightly-lined face was now filled with deep crevices.

For a few moments, silence filled the room right up to the vaulted ceiling. "Dad, what are you doing here?"

His father cleared his throat and attempted to straighten his shoulders. "Last time I checked I still owned this place." His voice was gruff. "Isn't a man allowed to visit his own property?"

Joshua gave a slight nod. Of course he wasn't here to visit his only son. Why would he ever do that? The man wasn't going to budge, so he wouldn't, either. "You won't own this property after tomorrow."

"I wouldn't be so sure, young man." He placed the hat gripped between his fingers on his head and turned toward the door.

"Wait! Why are you really here?"

His father spun around with a focused glare. His face flushed. He took one step closer and pointed his index finger in Joshua's face. "You're not going to bid on this inn. I want it out of the family. Do you hear me?"

"Family?" Joshua laughed out loud. "You don't know the meaning. The only family I ever had was Mom. She never wanted you to sell the inn. How could you tell her that was your plan when she was dying?"

"That's none of your business." His eyes were icy cold. "I'm just grateful Melissa called me and told me about your plan."

"So what are you going to do—cancel the auction?" He bit his lower lip. This couldn't be happening. Joshua didn't have a backup plan.

"That's exactly what I'm going to do."

"But then the inn will still be in the family." Joshua stated the fact.

"Not if I donate it to a charity." He ran his hand underneath his chin. "That's it. I'll give it to your mother's favorite—the Alzheimer's Association."

Joshua could barely catch his breath. Why was God allowing this man to ruin everything?

Be still, and know that I'm God.

A sense of peace filled his body when the verse his mother taught him at a young age entered his mind, a reminder to always trust Him, even when things didn't make sense. Joshua's shoulders relaxed. "Okay, Dad. It's your property, so I guess you have the right to do whatever you want with it."

His father's jaw muscle tightened for an instant, but then relaxed. "Yes, it is my property." He turned and yanked the door open, filling the room with a shot of winter air.

Joshua shivered at the sound of the slamming door. He moved to the window and watched his father drive away in his SUV. With heavy footsteps he headed out the door, wondering how on earth he'd ever tell Faith she'd lost her dream for the second time.

Later in the afternoon, Faith pressed her index fingers against her temples, attempting to keep the headache at bay. It wasn't working. Mrs. Watson had been kind enough to take care of lunch for the guests and then offered to pick up rotisserie chickens and some side dishes for dinner. She knew Faith was preoccupied with the auction. Now, holed up in her office in an attempt to get some paperwork accomplished, Faith was unable to maintain her focus. Her mind wandered to Joshua. Earlier, when she'd taken the casseroles up to the inn, she could tell he was upset. He'd raced past her without saying where he was headed. He hadn't even said goodbye. She could only assume the meeting with his father hadn't gone well.

A gentle knock on the door pulled her from her worries. "Faith, can I come in?"

She'd never been so relieved to hear her twin's voice. With the auction quickly approaching, she had so much she wanted to talk with her about.

The door slowly opened and her sister's smiling face appeared.

Faith pushed herself out of her chair. In desperate need of a hug, she met Joy in the center of the room. Standing on the circular Oriental rug once belonging to their grandmother, Faith was overcome with emotion.

"Why are you crying?"

She wished she knew. The past several weeks had been an emotional roller coaster. She was thrilled to think she'd become part owner of the Black Bear Inn, but the feelings swirling in her heart for Joshua left her with tremendous guilt. "There's so much I need to tell you." Faith headed toward the door and pushed it closed.

"Talk to me." Joy reached for her twin's hand and led her to the leather love seat situated between two windows. They both took a seat. Fifteen minutes later, her sister knew of Joshua's plan.

"I think I might be falling in love with Joshua." Faith blew out a heavy breath. "Did I just say that out loud?"

Joy laughed and clapped her hands together. "I knew it! Isn't it amazing how God works? He brought Joshua to you to provide you with the security you've longed for since Chris's death."

Faith had never thought the man who was trying to steal her only desire would be the one who'd make her dream come true. She ran her fingers through her hair. "Ever since Bella and Joshua were stranded in the storm, I've been feeling as though God's been trying to talk to me again."

"He's talking to you or you have you been speaking to Him?"

That night after the storm, when Joshua had brought her daughter home to her, she'd spent an hour in prayer. She had finally reignited the relationship she'd had with God before Chris died, confessing her anger toward Him. "Well, He's been talking all along, but I haven't been listening. I could never understand why He allowed the fire to steal my husband from me. Once I revealed my heart through prayer, everything became clear."

Joy reached out and hugged her only sister. "I'm so happy for you. No one deserves this more than you."

Faith nodded. "You were right. God did bring Joshua to me for a second chance. I just hope—" She couldn't stop thinking about the way Joshua had acted when she'd brought breakfast to the inn. "Never mind."

"What is it?"

"Joshua's father is here." And now Joshua was missing. Something was up. A shiver rattled her spine.

"I guess it makes sense. It is his property after all. Maybe he wants to make sure everything goes smoothly."

"That could be it, but their relationship is very contentious. According to Joshua, they don't speak to each other. Even at his mother's funeral, his father didn't acknowledge him."

"But his father has reached out to him. Maybe this is a good sign. Try not to worry so much." Joy rubbed her sister's arm.

When Joy's phone chimed, Faith waited as she responded to a text message.

Her twin slipped her phone into her purse. "I'm sorry, but I've got to get going. We have a faculty meeting scheduled this afternoon and Rose needs a ride. I'll be back to pick up Bella for her overnight. I got the kettle corn she likes so much and a stack of movies."

They said their goodbyes. Joy gave her a hug to reassure her that everything would work out.

Faith remained on the love seat for the next ten minutes. The whining and whirling of drills and the noise of nails being hammered entered through the cracked door. Renovations were moving along, but doubt consumed her. Had Mr. Carlson convinced his son a partnership was a bad idea? What if she'd lost her dream yet again?

Chapter Fifteen

Joshua paced the floor of his room like a nervous father waiting on the delivery of his first child. Earlier, he'd stormed off without a word to Faith. He'd jumped into his car to go for a drive. He needed to clear his head. Before he knew it, he'd found himself pulling over at a rest stop to text his father. He'd needed answers to so many questions. If he didn't address his father then, he probably never would. A knock at the door pulled him back into the moment. His stomach lurched.

"I wasn't sure if you'd come." Joshua moved out of the way as his father stepped inside and removed his hat.

"I said I would." The old man scanned the room.

The familiar scent of pipe tobacco lingered on his coat. "Here, let me take those." Joshua took the outerwear and hung them inside the coat closet. He turned to face the man who'd caused him a lifetime of pain and loneliness. "Can I get you something to drink?"

"No—I can't stay long," his father grumbled, avoiding any eye contact.

There was no warm and fuzzy from this man. There'd never been. Why would Joshua think anything would have changed after all these years? "There's a reason I asked you to come, so I'll get to the point." He stepped toward the desk and opened the drawer. Reaching inside, he pulled out a letter-size manila envelope and approached his father, who'd taken a seat in the leather chair in the corner of the room.

"What's this?" His father asked as he reached for the envelope.

"Open it."

His father did as Joshua requested. His eyes bulged as he scanned through each photograph in the envelope. His hands shook. Was he suffering from early Parkinson's disease? Of course not. Joshua hadn't seen them shake when they met earlier. It was the photos causing the tremors.

"Where did you get these?" He sprung from the chair unlike any old man Joshua had ever known. Loosening his tie, he locked his eyes, filled with fury, onto his only son. "Tell me! Now!"

Joshua had prepared himself for an angry response from his father, but he hadn't imagined this. The guy was livid. "Calm down—please."

He stepped toward his son, swatting the envelope into his face. "Don't tell me to settle down. I want an answer."

"At the inn…down in the basement. There were stacks of boxes. Faith didn't know who they belonged to so I took a look. Who's Jimmy, Dad?" Suddenly, this seemed like a bad idea. His father looked as though his head would explode. The redness initially filling his face seemed to be getting deeper in color.

"Don't ever mention that name again." He turned his attention back to the photo of him and Jimmy holding fishing poles as they stood beside a pond.

Were those tears he saw in the corner of his father's eye? No. It couldn't be. From the time Joshua was a little boy, his father had drilled into his head, "Real men never show their emotions and they certainly don't cry like babies."

His father slumped down into the chair, dropping the photos to the floor. As Joshua watched, the man who'd never showed any emotion, even at his wife's funeral, covered his face with his hands and released a lifetime of pent-up tears.

Joshua knelt down in front of the chair. He noticed his father's shoulders jerked in rapid movements. Placing his hand to stop the trembling, Joshua felt the bones where once there had been muscle. "Dad?"

The man peeled away his hands and looked at his son with tear-soaked eyes. "What have I done to you? I'm exactly like my father. Your entire life, I've treated you the same way he treated me." He ran his hand across his face. "How will I ever make this up to you?"

"Grandpa? What are you talking about, Dad?"

Joshua listened as his father talked about his painful past, recalling the demons from his childhood. How his own father had blamed him for the drowning death of his other son, Jimmy. Never offering forgiveness, no matter how many times he'd been asked. Joshua began to understand his father. His father was human after all. He'd treated Joshua the only way he knew how. Exactly how he'd been raised. The cycle of dysfunction had carried on to the next generation, but thankfully it would end today.

"It was my fault. I was the one who wanted to go skating. Jimmy didn't even want to go, but I forced him, my baby brother, and that day, his life ended when he fell through the ice." His sobs were uncontrollable. "It should have been me, not Jimmy." Years of pain and suffering flowed from the elderly man.

Joshua took two steps forward and, for the first time in his life, embraced his father. *The Lord our God is merciful and forgiving.* "It's okay, Dad. I forgive you."

His father pulled back and stared at his son with bloodshot eyes. "But why? I've treated you so badly—your entire life."

"It's what Mom taught me by taking me to church every Sunday."

A half smile parted the man's lips. "I miss her so much."

Joshua patted his father's shoulder. "So do I, Dad—every day."

After his father left, Joshua checked his messages on his phone. He smiled as he listened to a voice mail from Faith inviting him over for dinner. Since she didn't enjoy cooking, he assumed she was ordering a pizza or some takeout.

An hour later, after a quick shower and shave, Joshua walked in darkness to Faith's house. He felt as though the weight of the world had been removed from his shoulders. Making peace with his father had brought him more joy than he'd ever imagined. Much to Joshua's surprise, his father was actually a nice guy—and funny, too. He had told his son about the practical jokes he loved to play on his wife throughout their marriage. This had been a side of his father Joshua had never seen. He liked it. He'd been grateful when his father agreed to go through with the auction tomorrow. His father had finally understood why it was so important for Joshua to keep his promise to his mother. They'd hugged, said their goodbyes and even planned to meet for breakfast before the auction.

Since Faith knew nothing about his father's threats to take the inn off the auction block, he saw no need to mention it now, since everything was back on track for tomorrow.

It was after 8:00 p.m., so he gently knocked on the front door, in case Bella was already in bed. Of course, it was Friday night, so she might still be up. He hoped she was. After today, he needed a Bella fix.

His breath hitched when Faith opened the door, dressed in a red cashmere sweater and gray wool slacks. Her wavy caramel hair cascaded over her slender shoulders.

"Hello, Joshua. Please come in."

She cast a warm smile, causing his heart to hammer in his chest. Her fragrance smelled like sweet honeysuckle at the peak of summer, making him light-headed.

"I thought maybe we'd have dinner in the dining room."

"Sounds great to me." He looked around the room. "Where's the munchkin?"

"She's sleeping over at Joy's tonight. She'll bring her over to the community center in the morning. I still can't believe the auction is tomorrow." She turned and headed into the other room.

Joshua trailed behind her, enjoying the aroma drifting from the kitchen.

When he entered the dining room, his mouth dropped open. The lights were dim, but the warm glow from the candles on the elegantly set table emitted the perfect lighting for a romantic dinner.

Joshua turned to her. "Did you do all of this yourself?"

Her questioning brow signaled to him his words hadn't come out right. "I'm sorry. I didn't mean it that way. It's just the delicious smell coming from the kitchen and all this." He panned his hands in the air. "I didn't think you could cook."

A smile tugged at her lips. "I never really said I couldn't cook. I just don't like to, unless it's for someone special."

Apart from his mother, no one ever had uttered those thoughts about him. His heart soared. He'd made peace with his father, and now the most beautiful woman in the world thought he was special. His heart was overflowing with joy. "Would you like some apple cider before we have the salad?"

At that moment, he would have been happy with a stale piece of bread. He didn't want anything but to spend the rest of his days with this woman. Of course, he didn't want to be rude. "Sure, cider sounds great."

"Please, make yourself at home. I'll be right back with our drinks."

He watched as she glided out of the room. As he scanned the living room, the photographs on the mantel caught his eye. He stepped closer for a better look. He smiled at the pictures of her late husband dressed in his uniform. Joshua was happy Faith had realized leaving photos of Chris hidden away in the attic wasn't good for Bella or for herself. Another shot of Bella and Faith taken on a crisp autumn day warmed his heart. They were jumping into a large pile of golden-yellow leaves, wearing wide smiles. Next fall, could he be in the photograph, too? Warmth filled his chest at the thought.

After they finished their beverages and

salad, Faith surprised Joshua with a lovely meal of surf and turf.

"This is the most tender cut of meat I've ever eaten. It's melting in my mouth."

She nodded as she chewed a bite and then swallowed. "I'm glad you like it. I drove over to a quaint little town called Davis earlier. They have the best cuts of beef."

"I think you've been holding out on me."

"What do you mean?" She tapped her napkin to her pink lips.

"All of this time, you could have been doing all of the cooking for the guests. I think you're better at it than I am." He speared a piece of steak with his fork.

"Maybe so, but we probably wouldn't be sitting here together. We'd still be butting heads over the inn."

She was right. All the weeks they'd spent together in her cozy kitchen had brought them to this point. He was overwhelmed by the amount of trouble Faith had gone to in order to make this special meal for him. "Can I tell you something?"

"Of course."

"During my marriage, my ex never cooked a meal like this for me. In fact, she never made anything. Our dining usually consisted of delivery and premade dishes that only required reheating."

Faith placed her fork on her plate. Her eyes shimmered with flecks of gold when she looked up and met his gaze. "You're the first man I've made a meal for since Chris was killed. In fact, he was the only man I'd ever cooked for."

He reached over for her hand. "I don't know what I've done to deserve this, but please know how special this night is to me."

Following dinner, they feasted on a decadent chocolate mousse with a dollop of whipped cream. Then they headed into the kitchen to tackle the dishes.

"You really don't need to help with these. I can take care of it later," Faith said as she stacked some plates next to the sink.

"Nonsense—you did all the hard work, it's only fair I lend a hand."

Faith leaned up against the counter. "Can I ask you something, Joshua?"

"Sure—anything."

"Why are you so sure we'll get the inn? There might be other people, maybe real estate developers, who'll be interested in the property."

"It doesn't matter. I'll pay as much as I have to."

Her eyebrow arched. "Money's no object?"

He rested the oversize spoon on the plate next to the stove. Turning, he strolled toward her and their eyes held. She flinched when he took her hands and drew her closer to him. "No, it's not. I'm doing this for you…for us, and no one can stop me, Faith." He meant it, even if he had to beg his father to lend him the money.

It hadn't been planned, but when he was close enough to feel her warm breath on his face, he couldn't resist. Her lips were soft and tender just as he'd imagined them to be. Nothing else existed or mattered as their kiss deepened.

Faith pulled one hand free and gripped the edge of the countertop. A dreamy looked danced in her eyes. "I'm dizzy."

He pulled away. "Well, you better hold on because our ride is just getting started."

Later in the evening, back at the inn, Joshua cleared some of the auction documents off the desk and placed them into his leather briefcase. Since he'd left Faith's house, his feet hadn't touched the ground. Her dinner had been the perfect gift tonight, giving him a glimpse of what their future could be after tomorrow. He reached for his phone to check for messages, since he'd left it there when he went to dinner. He hadn't wanted any interruptions during his time with Faith. When he saw two voice-mail messages from Melissa, he deleted them without listening. Joshua pressed his back against the chair and released a breath, thankful to have that woman out of his life.

After Joshua left, Faith settled into her room with a cup of herbal tea and a romance novel. She laughed. Who needed to read this when her own life was starting to feel like one of these stories? When Joshua had kissed her, she'd stood speechless, hanging on to the counter. If she'd let go, she wasn't sure her weak legs could have kept her up right. She'd felt like a teenager with her first crush. Watching him work so hard over the past several weeks to keep the inn running as close to normal as possible, she'd known she was getting closer to realizing her dream. Thanks to that gorgeous man, her dream of owning the inn had turned into something even better—a chance for a new beginning. With her name on the deed, along with Joshua's signature, the inn would once again be a permanent home for her and Bella. The ground shifted under her feet when she realized she had fallen in love with Joshua Carlson. And deep inside her heart, she knew Chris would be okay with that.

At 9:00 a.m. the following morning, dressed in black slacks and a red turtleneck sweater,

Faith was ready for the auction, even though it wasn't scheduled to start until noon. With all the excitement in her head, she'd hardly slept, but she felt like a million dollars. Since Joshua planned to meet his father for breakfast and the Watsons were once again taking over meal preparations today—bless them both—Faith was able to sit down and enjoy a leisurely cup of coffee. She made a note to get a special gift for Mr. and Mrs. Watson. They'd done so much to help out after the fire at the inn.

Faith raised an eyebrow at the sound of a car door slamming out front. She rose from her chair when she heard footsteps approaching her door. She wasn't expecting anyone and rarely did she have unannounced visitors. Stepping into the family room, she took a sneak peek through the shudders. A white sedan had backed into the driveway.

A knock sounded as Faith tiptoed to the door. She took a quick look through the narrow windows on one side of the door and her breath hitched. Faith gripped the handle and slowly opened the door. A chill ran down her spine, but it wasn't from the outside air. "Melissa—what are you doing here?"

Forgoing an invitation inside, the woman breezed past Faith and entered the foyer. "It's freezing out there. I'd love a cup of coffee." She removed her long black wool coat and flung it over her arm.

Left with no choice, Faith decided to give the woman what she wanted. She sucked in a breath and prepared herself to be hospitable. "Sure, let's go into the kitchen. I just made a fresh pot."

The stiletto heels clicked behind Faith as they headed down the hall. Who wore those kinds of shoes when there was snow on the ground?

Faith filled two mugs and turned to Melissa. "How would you like it?"

"Sweet and creamy, like a milkshake," she laughed, brushing her red wavy hair away from her face. "So, where's my guy?"

My guy. "Excuse me?" Faith asked as she poured heavy cream, followed by two heaping teaspoons of sugar, into the coffee and gave it a swift stir. Yuck. How could she drink this? What was she, twelve?

"Joshua—I thought he'd be here cooking breakfast." She accepted her cup and took a sip. "Yum…this is perfect."

Still unclear why this woman had commandeered her kitchen and was now enjoying a hot beverage, Faith tried to think of an answer. She had an uneasy feeling. Joshua had told her Melissa was no longer working for him, so what had brought her here? "Do you have an appointment with him or something?" She couldn't help wondering what they'd have to meet about, especially when he'd seemed so angry the day she'd come to the inn. He hadn't talked much about it and Faith hadn't wanted to pry, but now she wished she had.

Melissa's pasted-on smile vanished, and her face turned stone-cold. "Look, I probably shouldn't be telling you this. Joshua won't be happy I did, but I'm here for the auction."

"Well, it is a public event. You're more than welcome to come and observe." Not that she wanted her there. In fact, she couldn't wait to get this woman out of her kitchen.

An odd sound resembling a laugh escaped Melissa's mouth, but Faith thought it was more like a malicious noise uttered by one of Cinderella's stepsisters in the movie that Bella often watched. "I'll be attending the auction, but I'll certainly not be observing."

The knot in her stomach, which had appeared as soon as she'd opened the door earlier, expanded into what felt like a beach ball. "Do you have a client who's interested in the inn?"

Melissa smirked. "I guess there's no point in keeping it a secret any longer. You'll find out soon enough." She smoothed her hair with fingernails painted fire-engine red. "I'm going to bid on the inn and, trust me, I'll be the one who walks away with the deed to the property—not you."

Faith eyed the woman, not sure if she was telling the truth or playing some sort of game to get back at Joshua. Emotions bubbled like fiery lava. This property belonged to her, it was part of her heritage. She wouldn't let it go without a fight. "Don't be so sure, Melissa." Who did Melissa think she was, coming into the picture just when she and Joshua had made peace and possibly had a future together?

"Trust me. I've got more money than you or anyone who might attend the auction. I guess Joshua never mentioned I inherited a fortune when my grandfather passed away."

Faith's heart hammered inside her chest. Was this true? After all this, would she really lose the inn to this heartless woman? "Why are you doing this? Are you trying to get back at Joshua for letting you go?"

Melissa rolled her eyes. "I'm doing this for him. His mother loved this place. That's why it means so much to him. He's nervous he'll be outbid by you or another investor, so I've decided to purchase it for us—for our future together."

Together? Future? What on earth was she talking about? What about her future? Just last night, it had seemed so bright.

"Oh, you poor thing, you didn't know." Melissa's lips pursed. "Since you and Joshua have been spending so much time together, I assumed he'd told you already."

Her jaw tightened. "Told me what?"

"The only reason he cut business ties with me was so we could finally be together." She paused and locked eyes with Faith. "As a couple. We've known each other all our lives and finally, after all these years, there's nothing standing in our way. We're in love, sweetheart." Her eyes glittered like daggers.

How could this be true? Melissa wasn't his type. Faith had thought she was, but maybe she'd been wrong. What about the kiss they'd shared? Her stomach rolled over when she thought of her daughter. Bella would be heartbroken, not only to lose her home, but also Joshua.

"Did you hear me?" Melissa took a step closer, her perfume putrid. "Joshua and I will be together, not you and him."

Melissa headed toward the door just when Faith thought she could no longer hold back her tears. She abruptly stopped and turned around. "I know you think your sweet little girl has won him over—actually, it's kind of pathetic that'd you have to use your daughter to get a man, but whatever, it's me he's always loved—just remember that."

Faith slumped into the kitchen chair as the car's engine roared in the distance. She dropped her head into her hands and the tears gushed. What about last night? The tender kiss she'd shared with Joshua. He'd made a promise to her and offered a new beginning. But why?

Minutes later, she wiped her eyes. With heaviness in her limbs, she lifted herself from the chair. Drawn to the photo of her husband on the wall, she willed her weighted legs to move toward it. "I'm so sorry, Chris. I pushed you into becoming a firefighter. I thought good benefits and a pension would provide me with the security I craved growing up. Security isn't about money. I know that now." She swallowed hard and placed her fingertips on the photo. "I'm sorry I couldn't make your dream come true." She turned and headed toward her bedroom to get undressed. The auction would go on without her. As she crawled underneath the warmth of her grandmother's afghan her stomach rolled over as she realized her future had once again been stripped away.

Chapter Sixteen

The parking lot of the community center was about half-full when Joshua zipped into an available end spot. Obviously, the townspeople were interested in the future of the Black Bear. He hoped there wouldn't be too many out-of-town investors interested in placing a bid. It didn't really matter—he was determined to make Faith's dream come true, no matter the cost.

Inside, a sea of people filled the main meeting room. Rows of folding chairs were lined up in front of the podium. He spied Joy and Bella in the first row. Where was Faith? She should be here by now.

There was a hum of muffled voices in the room as he worked his way through a gathering of men dressed in business suits. Odd. No one usually wore suits around here, except to church on Sunday. His stomach twisted as he realized he wouldn't be the only person placing a bid.

"Mr. Joshua!" Bella yelled as she bounced in her seat. "Sit next to me."

"Hello, ladies. I've got to take care of a few things, but I'll be back to join you." He glanced at Joy. "Where's Faith?"

"I haven't spoken with her this morning. I tried calling her cell and home phone, but there wasn't any answer. I just assumed she'd already left with you." Joy's face was awash with concern.

"No, I had breakfast this morning with my father. I haven't seen or talked with her since last night." Thoughts of the kiss they'd shared calmed his nerves, but only for a moment. "Do you think I should run by the cottage?"

Joy shook her head. "I don't think that's necessary. She's probably running a few of her normal Saturday morning errands before she heads over."

A short and stout gentleman with a receding hairline approached the microphone. "Testing, testing." He tapped twice.

Joshua's pulse race as tiny beads of perspiration dotted his brow. The auction was ready to start. He'd feel a lot better if Faith was here. He removed his phone from his jacket pocket and pulled up his contacts. He tapped Call, praying she'd pick up. His shoulders slumped when the call went straight to voice mail. A quick glance at his watch rattled his nerves. Where was she?

With his mouth parched, Joshua headed toward the concession table for a drink of water. He handed the elderly woman a dollar bill and unscrewed the top. Taking a long swig, he choked when he spotted Melissa sashaying across the room, heading straight toward him.

Her arms were open when he felt her breath. "I've been looking all over for you."

Quickly, he stepped back to avoid any contact. His frustration mounted. Why couldn't she take a hint? "What are you doing here?"

"I'm here for you—for us." She shot him a dreamy gaze.

"I told you before, there's no us. You shouldn't have come, Melissa. Please leave."

"I can't do that, not until I buy the inn."

His ears pounded. What had she just said?

She reached for his arm, but his reaction was too quick. "I know how much the Black Bear means to you, so I'm going to buy it for you. Apparently, there are many other investors who could possibly outbid you. But with my grandfather's money, I can go higher than anyone else."

He blinked his eyes several times, wishing

that this was just a bad dream. But Melissa still stood in front of him with hopeful eyes. His mother had always told him honesty was the best policy, so he took a chance. "Look, Melissa, it's an extremely generous gesture, but I can't accept it."

"But why?"

"Because I'm in love with Faith. We've pooled our funds in order to buy the inn today. I want to start a life with her and Bella."

"No! You can't! She's not right for you." Her cheeks flushed. "She'll never love you the way I do."

This was worse than he'd thought. She wasn't going to take no for an answer, but he had to make her understand before she ruined everything. "But don't you see? I don't love you, Melissa, and I never have." Yes, his words were cruel—but he'd been left with no other options.

She glared at him in silence. The buzz from the growing crowd filled the room as he waited for her response. "Then where is she? If you're joining forces, why isn't she here with you?"

That was the question of the hour. He gave the room a quick scan in hopes of seeing Faith in the crowd. Still missing. "I don't know. I haven't been able to reach her. She's probably running some errands."

"Doubtful," Melissa spoke, shaking her hair away from her face.

"What's that supposed to mean?"

"I don't think she's out running errands. If she's like any other heartbroken woman, she's home in her pajamas eating a half gallon of rocky road ice cream."

"What in the world are you talking about? She's not heartbroken."

When Melissa inched just a little closer, her face lacked any emotion. "Don't be so sure. I paid her a visit this morning."

"You what—"

The loud squealing of the sound system caused the people to settle into their chairs.

"We're not done here," Joshua proclaimed as he hurried to his seat. He wanted nothing more than to leave the auction and get to Faith's house as fast as possible. But he couldn't leave. There was no way on earth he'd allow Melissa to ruin his plans.

Settled into his chair, he watched in confusion as his father stepped behind the microphone, his face stony. Why was he here? According to his father, there was no reason for him to attend.

RC looked strong and much more powerful than he had in his son's room yesterday. Joshua had an uneasy feeling.

His father cleared his throat and leaned forward. "I'm sorry you've wasted your time, but there won't be an auction today. The Black Bear Inn is not for sale. Not today—not ever." With those words, he turned and headed toward the door from which he'd emerged.

The crowd murmured, but it didn't silence the gasp escaping from Joshua's lips.

Joy turned to him. "What's going on, Joshua?"

That was what he'd like to know. Joshua bolted from his chair and sprinted toward the door. He spotted his father walking across the common area, heading straight for the exit.

"Dad, wait!" Joshua ran across the room, bumping into two teenage boys and not taking the time to apologize. His father ignored him and continued toward the door. Joshua caught up to him and grabbed his arm. "What do you think you're doing?"

The man turned to his son, his face emotionless. "I'm not selling the inn."

Joshua's face burned. He'd thought they'd made their peace yesterday. How could his father do this?

"Mr. Joshua!"

The two men turned toward the screaming child as Bella ran at top speed across the room. When she reached them, Joshua knelt down in front of her. "Go back with your Aunt Joy,

Bella. I'll be there in a few minutes. I need to speak with my father."

Tears streamed down the little girl's rosy cheeks. "You're ruining everything," she said as she looked up at Joshua's father. "Mr. Joshua was buying the inn for my mommy, so we can be a family. He was going to be my daddy," she wailed.

Joshua's heart was breaking, but his anger toward his father bubbled over like an unattended pot of boiling water. He scooped Bella into his arms and she buried her faced into his shoulder. When he glanced at the door, he saw Melissa and Joy watching.

"Please don't cry, child."

When his father spoke in a soft and concerned tone, Joshua wasn't sure if it was really his words. He examined the elderly man and was surprised once again by what he saw. Tears were forming in the corners of his dark eyes, something he'd seen for the first time yesterday when his father spoke of Jimmy. Crying was a sign of weakness and not permitted in the Carlson household—so his father had always said.

Joshua rubbed Bella's back as she continued to sob. He watched as his father's expression continued to soften.

The older man cleared his throat. "Can we talk alone?"

His father's request caught him off guard. Joshua placed Bella on the ground. Her tears slowly subsided. "Sweetie, why don't you run along?" He pointed in her aunt's direction. "I'll be with you in a few minutes."

With her head down, Bella walked at a snail's pace toward Joy. She stopped in her tracks and turned. "Please, Mr. Joshua's daddy, don't take away my mommy's dream." She continued toward the door.

"Yesterday, I thought you understood why the inn was so important to me, Dad. Why would you take it off the auction block?"

His father turned his gaze to Joshua. "Let me make it up to you."

Joshua wasn't sure what "it" was. There'd been so many incidents in his life that could have scarred him emotionally if he hadn't learned to trust God and the power of forgiveness. If only his father had done the same, perhaps their relationship would have been different.

"I want to make up for every horrible thing I've ever done to you, son." His father hung his head in shame. "There were so many... I know that."

Joshua couldn't argue with him. It was the truth and he was grateful his father had realized it.

"I'll have my attorney draw up the papers in the morning."

"Papers?"

His father nodded. "A deed transfer. I want to gift the inn over to you and the child's mother. It's what your mother would want." He paused for a moment. "It's what I want."

Joshua watched as his father left the building. He prayed in silence. He asked for peace for the man who had endured so much pain as a child. Today, his father had taken a big step in repairing their relationship. Joshua smiled, knowing his mother would be so happy.

The joy surging through his body came to a screeching halt. Faith.

He turned with a jerk and bolted for the door. Inside his car, he placed his key into the ignition and prayed to God Melissa hadn't ruined everything.

Listlessly, Faith peeled herself out of her bed. She trudged into the bathroom and flipped the switch. A quick glance in the mirror revealed a face in dire need of washing. The mascara she'd so carefully applied early this morning had run tracks down her cheeks, providing evidence of the hours of tears shed. She reached for her cleanser in an attempt to wash away the hurt.

She changed into her favorite comfy sweat

suit and headed into the kitchen. A nice cup of herbal tea was in order. Placing the kettle on the stovetop, she pulled a mug from the cabinet. Somehow she'd have to get the bombshell Melissa had dropped out of her head. She had a lot of things to figure out. The first being where would she and Bella live? There was no way now she'd stay on and work for Joshua. The thought of seeing him and Melissa together as a couple made her stomach wrench.

Settled down at the kitchen table, she gazed out the window toward the inn. She smiled as she studied the tree she and Joy had loved to climb as children. Taking a sip of her tea, she practically gagged when once again the tears flowed. *How could You have let this happen, God? I thought You and I were good now?*

Moments later, the sound of a car's engine and a door slamming pulled Faith back to her grim reality.

"Faith! Open the door!"

Joshua's fist pounding on the door prompted Faith to spring from her chair. No. What was he doing here? He should be at the auction with Melissa. By now, the property belonged to them. Her heart sank at the thought. She couldn't see him now—or ever.

"Please, I need to talk to you."

His words sounded desperate, but she didn't

care. She couldn't. He'd hurt her too badly. She'd opened her heart to a man, something she hadn't done since Chris had died, and gotten wounded.

She stood cowering in the corner, with her arms wrapped tight around her waist. *Please, make him go away.*

"Fine. I'll stay out here all day. In fact, I'll just sleep out here. I'm not going to leave, Faith, not until you open the door and let me explain."

Ten minutes later, she hadn't moved. Silence beyond the door made her wonder if he'd finally given up. There'd been no sounds of his car starting, but he could have walked up to the inn. Curiosity got the best of her and she crept toward the window. Her chest tightened when she spotted Joshua sitting on her porch. His head leaned forward into his strong hands.

What could she do? She certainly couldn't let him sit out there all night. He'd freeze to death. Plus, Joy would be bringing Bella home since the auction was over. Those thoughts propelled her to the door. With a tight grip, she jerked it open.

"What do you want, Joshua?" She bit down on her lip to keep the tears from a repeat performance.

He sprung to his feet with a smile, causing her heart to melt. From the moment she'd first seen him, the day he rescued Bella in the forest, his good looks had made her legs unsteady.

"Thank you for opening the door. May I please come inside?"

Her mind told her no, but her heart couldn't get into agreement, so she moved aside. "Yes, come in. Bella will be home soon, so please, let's make this quick."

Joshua stepped inside and she thought she'd drop to her knees when the familiar sweet smell of peppermint created a flood of memories. From the start, it was the one thing Bella had loved about him. Perhaps she found comfort in the aroma.

"Can I get you some tea?" The moment she offered, she wanted to take it back.

His smile was warm as he nodded. "That sounds nice." He took a seat at the table.

When the kettle sounded, Faith's hand quivered as she poured the water and bobbed the tea bags in each mug. She carried the beverages to the table, amazed she hadn't spilled any.

"Thank you." He smiled and lifted the cup to his lips, blowing softly.

Melissa's words tore at her heart. Faith wanted to run from the table and let the tears gush. If she hadn't been so emotionally exhausted, she might have. "Remember? Bella will be home soon."

He placed his drink on the table. A pained look filled his eyes. "I know Melissa was here earlier."

A quiet came over the room as Faith did everything in her power to keep her emotions in check. "That's true."

"Whatever she might have said to you—don't believe it." A deeper knowing filled his eyes. "Melissa is living in some sort of fantasy world. She believes we belong together, but it couldn't be any further from the truth."

"She seemed pretty convincing to me." Fear caused her to hesitate, but she had to know the answer. "Did she buy the inn for you at the auction today?" A tear streamed down her cheek.

Joshua reached across the table and placed his hand on her face. "There was no auction. My father canceled it."

For a second, Faith thought the nightmare was over. She and Bella would continue to live in the cottage and everything would remain the same. But who was she kidding? Nothing would be the same without Joshua in her life. "Why would he do that?"

"He's gifting the deed over to us, sweetie."

"To you and Melissa?" Another piece of her heart crumbled.

Joshua stood up from the table and walked

to her side. He took her hand to guide her to her feet. "No, to us—me and you."

Tears stung her eyes. She tried to blink them back before he noticed, but it didn't work. "What about Melissa? She told me you were in love with her." She paused to catch her breath. "The two of you were going to start a life together at the inn."

Joshua placed both of his hands on the sides of her face. "Listen to me. The only people who will be starting a life at the Black Bear Inn are you, me and Bella. But there is one condition."

Faith's head was spinning as she tried to understand what was happening and what had happened to Melissa. But the second he placed his lips onto hers, she didn't care. The only thing that mattered was Joshua still loved her and Bella, and all of her dreams were coming true. She forced herself to pull away from his gentle kiss, savoring the taste. She threw him a questioning eye. "So, what's the condition?"

He flashed the smile she'd fallen in love with. "From now on, I only have to cook for you and Bella."

"You've got a deal."

Epilogue

"Come on, slowpoke." Faith glanced over her shoulder as fat snowflakes splattered against her exposed cheeks. She inhaled the invigorating mountain air.

"Who are you calling a slowpoke? Remember, this is my first time cross-country skiing."

She dug her poles into the snow-covered trail, gliding along with ease.

"Show-off," Joshua shouted as he fell farther behind.

Faith laughed at the man who had given her the greatest gift ever—security for her and Bella. Not to mention the promise of something more.

When Melissa had shown up and announced she and Joshua were in love, Faith had thought all hope was lost. Instead, Joshua had presented her with a deed to the only place that she'd ever consider home.

The weeks had passed in a whirlwind of meetings with developers and architects, filling their days. Finally, they'd celebrated the groundbreaking for the new Black Bear Ski Resort and Spa.

Joshua's vision was becoming a reality. The weather had cooperated, so construction moved along at a brisk pace. She and Bella were still living in the cottage, and Joshua had taken up permanent residence at the inn. Eventually, she and her daughter would move into the inn, but not until the renovations were complete. Soon they'd break ground on the first phase of condominiums and a larger inn for those guests who preferred more pampering.

Joshua had given her the biggest surprise when he'd told her of his plans to restore the inn back to its original state. He wanted the house to be exactly like it had been when Faith and Joy went to live with their grandparents, after their parents were killed.

"Can we please take a break?" Joshua pleaded.

Up ahead, a couple of large boulders covered in a light dusting of snow looked rather inviting to Faith. After an hour and a half on the trail, she was ready for a little break herself. With a shuffling motion, she arrived at the rocks and brushed away the snow. She flopped down and took off her skis. Smiling, she watched as Joshua slowly made his way toward her. Unable to peel her eyes off the gorgeous man, she stifled a laugh as he struggled with his footing.

When the sun popped out from behind the low-lying clouds, she untied her red scarf and pulled it loose from her neck. She tipped her face to the sun and thanked God for this day. Although she and Joshua had been spending every waking minute together, this was their first opportunity to get away from the construction and relax a bit. But judging from the painful look on his face, she wasn't sure he was too relaxed.

Joshua huffed and puffed his way up to the rocks and dropped his poles into the snow. "This is exhausting. It's a lot different from snow skiing."

The scent of peppermint made her dizzy when he took a seat on her boulder. "Hey, this was your idea, remember?" It seemed a lifetime ago that she'd cared for him after his skiing accident. So much had changed, and she couldn't remember the last time her heart was this full.

He nodded and removed his gloves. "You're right. I don't know what I was thinking," Joshua laughed and reached for her hand. He removed her right glove and pressed his lips against her skin.

She shivered.

Concern crept across his face. "Are you cold?"

The snow showers had stopped and the sun shone brightly. "No—just happy." She smiled.

They cuddled closer, taking in the sight of the snow-capped mountains surrounding them. Off in a clearing, a gathering of deer foraged for their next meal.

"Don't you love it out here?" Faith took in a deep breath and filled her lungs with the crisp mountain air. "There's no other place I'd rather be." She turned to the man who'd made all of her dreams possible. "Or anyone else I'd rather be with."

He cleared his throat and bent over to remove his skis.

The rumbling sounds of a motor in the distance, but moving closer, filled the air.

Faith turned. "It sounds like some snowmobilers headed this way. There goes our peaceful little sanctuary." She squinted in the direction of the noise and saw Mr. Watson powering up the trail with someone on the back of the recreational vehicle. *Bella.* She was supposed to be with Joy.

"Hi, Mommy!" She grinned as the elderly man glided up to the rocks.

"Bella, what are you doing up here?"

Joshua nodded to Mr. Watson. "Give me about twenty minutes." He lifted Bella off the back of the snowmobile and perched her on the boulder next to her mother.

"I'll be back," the old man yelled over the motor as he peeled off.

Faith's eyebrow arched. "What's going on?"

"Mr. Joshua wanted to ask us something, Mommy."

When the man she loved dropped to one knee, Faith's heart hammered from beneath her snowsuit. Her daughter squealed. Was this really happening? Or was she dreaming?

"Faith, Bella." He looked at both of them. "I've brought you here to tell you something. Since God brought you into my life, I've never been happier. You each have a special place in my heart and I love you both."

"We love you, too, Mr. Joshua," Bella blurted out and both adults chuckled.

He reached deep inside the pocket of his gray jacket and pulled out a small blue velvet box.

Faith could hardly breathe as he placed it in front of her and her daughter. At that moment, Chris's voice spoke to her heart... *You have to move on, Faith. It's time.*

Joshua's eyes glistened as he opened the box, revealing two rings. "Faith, Bella, I want us to be a family, will you marry me?"

Before Faith could even answer, her daughter sprung off the rock and straight into Joshua's arms. "I knew you were meant to be my daddy!"

Tears peppered Faith's eyes. Bella would be raised with a father, just as Chris wanted.

Joshua looked at Faith as she wiped her eyes. "Does this mean yes?"

When he stood holding Bella in his arms, she rose, her legs like a newborn calf's. Faith reached for his hand. Unable to speak, she could only smile and nod.

"Are you sure?"

She cast a weightless gaze at the man who was offering her and her daughter another chance at happily-ever-after. Love, safety and security...all she'd ever wanted for herself and Bella. She swallowed the lump in her throat. "I've never been more certain of anything."

Bella turned to him. "I'm sure, too, Mr. Joshua—oops, I mean Daddy."

* * * * *

*If you enjoyed A Father For Bella, be sure to
look for Jill Weatherholt's previous title
SECOND CHANCE ROMANCE*

*And check out these other emotionally
gripping and wonderful stories*

*HER COWBOY REUNION
by Ruth Logan Herne
THE RANCHER'S SURPRISE DAUGHTER
by Jill Lynn
MEANT-TO-BE BABY
by Lois Richer
THE DEPUTY'S UNEXPECTED FAMILY
by Patricia Johns*

Available now from Love Inspired!

*Find more great reads at
www.LoveInspired.com*

Dear Reader,

When I was a little girl, the sound of late night sirens sent me running to my parents' bedroom, seeking refuge underneath their covers. I feared the emergency vehicle was on its way to our house.

Unlike Faith Brennan, who experienced the devastating loss of her firefighter husband that resulted in a fear of hospitals and triggered panic attacks, my distress was unfounded. In time, I outgrew that anxiety, but others took root.

Fear seeps into all of our lives, weaving itself around our heart and mind. It comes in many forms, both big and small. Left unchecked, it can interfere with our daily living and prevent us from being in the will of God. Living apprehensive of what *might* happen can often create more anxiety than actually facing the fear head on.

The longer we allow fear to linger, the more difficult it is to break free. Faith and Joshua released their fears, and you can, too. Make a decision to step out in faith and live the life God has in store for you. Remember, He is greater than any obstacle you may be facing.

Thank you so much for visiting Whispering Slopes. Having the opportunity to write a second Love Inspired story, set in a fictional town of the Shenandoah Valley, has been another dream come true.

One of the best things about being a writer is connecting with readers, so be sure to sign up to receive my bimonthly blog posts via email @jillweatherholt.wordpress.com or email me at authorjillweatherholt@gmail.com. You can also find me on Facebook @jillweatherholtauthor and Twitter @jillweatherholt.

Jill

Get 4 FREE REWARDS!

We'll send you 2 FREE Books plus 2 FREE Mystery Gifts.

Love Inspired® Suspense books feature Christian characters facing challenges to their faith... and lives.

FREE Value Over $20

YES! Please send me 2 FREE Love Inspired® Suspense novels and my 2 FREE mystery gifts (gifts are worth about $10 retail). After receiving them, if I don't wish to receive any more books, I can return the shipping statement marked "cancel." If I don't cancel, I will receive 4 brand-new novels every month and be billed just $5.24 each for the regular-print edition or $5.74 each for the larger-print edition in the U.S., or $5.74 each for the regular-print edition or $6.24 each for the larger-print edition in Canada. That's a savings of at least 13% off the cover price. It's quite a bargain! Shipping and handling is just 50¢ per book in the U.S. and 75¢ per book in Canada*. I understand that accepting the 2 free books and gifts places me under no obligation to buy anything. I can always return a shipment and cancel at any time. The free books and gifts are mine to keep no matter what I decide.

Choose one: ☐ **Love Inspired® Suspense**
Regular-Print
(153/353 IDN GMY5)

☐ **Love Inspired® Suspense**
Larger-Print
(107/307 IDN GMY5)

LIS18

Name (please print)

Address   Apt. #

City   State/Province   Zip/Postal Code

Mail to the **Reader Service:**
IN U.S.A.: P.O. Box 1341, Buffalo, NY 14240-8531
IN CANADA: P.O. Box 603, Fort Erie, Ontario L2A 5X3

Want to try two free books from another series? Call 1-800-873-8635 or visit www.ReaderService.com.

Get 4 FREE REWARDS!

We'll send you 2 FREE Books plus 2 FREE Mystery Gifts.

Harlequin® Heartwarming™ Larger-Print books feature traditional values of home, family, community and most of all—love.

FREE
Value Over
$20

YES! Please send me 2 FREE Harlequin® Heartwarming™ Larger-Print novels and my 2 FREE mystery gifts (gifts worth about $10 retail). After receiving them, if I don't wish to receive any more books, I can return the shipping statement marked "cancel." If I don't cancel, I will receive 4 brand-new larger-print novels every month and be billed just $5.49 per book in the U.S. or $6.24 per book in Canada. That's a savings of at least 19% off the cover price. It's quite a bargain! Shipping and handling is just 50¢ per book in the U.S. and 75¢ per book in Canada*. I understand that accepting the 2 free books and gifts places me under no obligation to buy anything. I can always return a shipment and cancel at any time. The free books and gifts are mine to keep no matter what I decide.

161/361 IDN GMY3

Name (please print)

Address   Apt. #

City   State/Province   Zip/Postal Code

Mail to the Reader Service:
IN U.S.A.: P.O. Box 1341, Buffalo, NY 14240-8531
IN CANADA: P.O. Box 603, Fort Erie, Ontario L2A 5X3

Want to try two free books from another series? Call 1-800-873-8635 or visit www.ReaderService.com.

---

*Terms and prices subject to change without notice. Prices do not include applicable taxes. Sales tax applicable in N.Y. Canadian residents will be charged applicable taxes. Offer not valid in Quebec. This offer is limited to one order per household. Books received may not be as shown. Not valid for current subscribers to Harlequin Heartwarming Larger-Print books. All orders subject to approval. Credit or debit balances in a customer's account(s) may be offset by any other outstanding balance owed by or to the customer. Please allow 4 to 6 weeks for delivery. Offer available while quantities last.

Your Privacy—The Reader Service is committed to protecting your privacy. Our Privacy Policy is available online at www.ReaderService.com or upon request from the Reader Service. We make a portion of our mailing list available to reputable third parties that offer products we believe may interest you. If you prefer that we not exchange your name with third parties, or if you wish to clarify or modify your communication preferences, please visit us at www.ReaderService.com/consumerschoice or write to us at Reader Service Preference Service, P.O. Box 9062, Buffalo, NY 14240-9062. Include your complete name and address.

HWI8

HOME *on the* RANCH

YES! Please send me the **Home on the Ranch Collection** in Larger Print. This collection begins with 3 FREE books and 2 FREE gifts in the first shipment. Along with my 3 free books, I'll also get the next 4 books from the Home on the Ranch Collection, in LARGER PRINT, which I may either return and owe nothing, or keep for the low price of $5.24 U.S./ $5.89 CDN each plus $2.99 for shipping and handling per shipment*. If I decide to continue, about once a month for 8 months I will get 6 or 7 more books, but will only need to pay for 4. That means 2 or 3 books in every shipment will be FREE! If I decide to keep the entire collection, I'll have paid for only 32 books because 19 books are FREE! I understand that accepting the 3 free books and gifts places me under no obligation to buy anything. I can always return a shipment and cancel at any time. My free books and gifts are mine to keep no matter what I decide.

268 HCN 3760 468 HCN 3760

Name _____ (PLEASE PRINT)

Address _____ Apt. #

City _____ State/Prov. _____ Zip/Postal Code

Signature (if under 18, a parent or guardian must sign)

Mail to the **Reader Service:**
IN U.S.A.: P.O. Box 1341, Buffalo, New York 14240-8531
IN CANADA: P.O. Box 603, Fort Erie, Ontario L2A 5X3

* Terms and prices subject to change without notice. Prices do not include applicable taxes. Sales tax applicable in NY. Canadian residents will be charged applicable taxes. This offer is limited to one order per household. All orders subject to approval. Credit or debit balances in a customer's account(s) may be offset by any other outstanding balance owed by or to the customer. Please allow 3 to 4 weeks for delivery. Offer available while quantities last. Offer not available to Quebec residents.

HRCBPA18R

READERSERVICE.COM

Manage your account online!

- Review your order history
- Manage your payments
- Update your address

> ### We've designed the Reader Service website just for you.

Enjoy all the features!

- Discover new series available to you, and read excerpts from any series.
- Respond to mailings and special monthly offers.
- Browse the Bonus Bucks catalog and online-only exculsives.
- Share your feedback.

Visit us at:

ReaderService.com